PRAISE FOR THE WRITING
OF FRED WAITZKIN

Anything Is Good

"*Anything Is Good*, based on the true story of a brilliant and beleaguered childhood friend, offers a deeply affecting dive into the lives of the unhoused. Its shifting perspective and changing narrative voice builds to a clarion call for greater empathy and understanding."

—Geraldine Brooks, Pulitzer Prize–winning author

"*Anything Is Good* is the best portrait of homelessness I've read since George Orwell's *Down and Out in Paris and London*. Superbly written."

—Gabriel Byrne

Searching for Bobby Fischer

"[A] gem of a book . . . [its] quest is beautifully resolved."

—Christopher Lehmann-Haupt, *The New York Times*

"A vivid, passionate, and disquieting book."   —Martin Amis,
The Times Literary Supplement

"I've seldom been so captivated by a book."   —Tom Stoppard

"Under the spreading chess-nut tree there have been many chess books. To my mind this is the best."   —Cleveland Amory

"A truly magical book."   —Anthony Quinn

Deep Water Blues

"Fred Waitzkin effortlessly recreates a singular world with uncanny insight and humor. His language is remarkable for its clarity and simplicity. Yet his themes are profound. This is like sitting by a fire with a master storyteller whose true power is in the realm of imagination and magic."

—Gabriel Byrne

"Since I was a child, the desolate out islands of the Bahamas have been a home, none more dear than the shark-infested, storm ravaged, cursed utopia of Rum Cay. . . . *Deep Water Blues* churns with the beauty, desperation, violence, and yearning of those fighting to survive on a speck of land in an eternal sea. As a reader, I am on fire. As a son, I could not be more proud."

—Josh Waitzkin

"Loved this book. I could not put it down. A lifetime of memories of my own fishing these same waters."

—Mark Messier, hockey legend

"*Deep Water Blues* does what all fine literature aspires for—it transports readers to another time and place, in this case, to a sleepy, lush island deep in the Bahamas. Fred Waitzkin writes about life, sex, and violence with aplomb, and Bobby Little is a tragic hero fit for the Greek myths. Hope to see everyone on Rum Cay soon."

—Matt Gallagher, author of *Youngblood*

"*Deep Water* Blues has the ease and compelling charm of a yarn spun late in the evening, the sun gone down and the shadows gathering in."

—Colin Barret, author of *Young Skins*

The Last Marlin

"A remarkably ambitious and satisfying memoir."

—*The New York Times Book Review*

"When Fred Waitzkin was younger, he thought he had it in him to be a good writer. He was right. This memoir of growing up is passionate, often very funny, very tender, and thoroughly engrossing." —Peter Jennings

"Finding purity in the rarefied world of big-game fishing was Ernest Hemingway's forte, and he imbued it with transcendent significance. Fred does the same in *The Last Marlin*, but in far more human terms."

—John Clemans, editor, *Motor Boating & Sailing*

"Though there is much sorrow and confusion on these pages there is great beauty—a nearly profligate amount of it—almost everywhere you look . . . clearly one of a kind and deeply moving." —*Jewish Exponent*

The Dream Merchant

"Waitzkin offers a singular and haunting morality tale, sophisticated, literary and intelligent. Thoroughly entertaining. Deeply imaginative. Highly recommended." —*Kirkus Reviews* (starred review)

"Fred Waitzkin took me into a world of risk and violence and salvation that I was loath to relinquish. It's a great novel." —Sebastian Junger

"*The Dream Merchant* is a masterpiece. A cross between *Death of a Salesman* and *Heart of Darkness*. I believe that in the not-too-distant future we will be referring to Waitzkin's novel as a classic." —Anita Shreve

Mortal Games

"Waitzkin captures better than anyone—including Kasparov himself in his own memoir—the various sides of this elusive genius."

—*The Observer*

"Compelling." —*GQ*

Strange Love

"*In Strange Love*, real life ends and imagination begins, in a broken-down bar in a forgotten place—that is where you'll find Fred Waitzkin, fishing for stories." —Marion Winik, *Newsday*

"Fred Waitzkin is always a hot, smart, irresistible read . . . in his new book the heroic characters—and Waitzkin is always laying bets one way or another on heroism—are women." —Harvey Blume, literary critic

"Engaging and affecting . . . intense." —*English Plus Language Blog*

"Moving and memorable." —*The Vineyard Gazette*

Anything Is Good

ANYTHING IS GOOD

Fred Waitzkin

OPEN ROAD
INTEGRATED MEDIA
NEW YORK

ISBN: 978-1-5040-9403-0

Published in 2025 by Open Road Integrated Media, Inc.
180 Maiden Lane
New York, NY 10038
www.openroadmedia.com

for

Bonnie

Katya

Josh

Desi

Jack

Charlie

I could not have written this novel without the story telling gift and unsettling insights of Ralph Silverman.

Anything Is Good

Part I

As a teenager, I dreamed of playing conga drums with Herbie Mann or writing novels like Jack Kerouac. I decided, after college, or even before, to hitchhike the country, sleeping in box cars or beside the road, enjoying women while gathering experiences for my best-selling books. For several years, I was on fire with this homeless plan. My best friend, Ralph, patronized my adolescent fantasies with a throaty chuckle. He had his eye on larger game, or at least that's what I thought. Ralph wouldn't tell me his aspirations, not then, except for a few bits and snatches, perhaps because he thought I wouldn't understand.

Ralph was smarter than I was, smarter than anyone I knew in our Bronx high school. He was already dipping into the works of Kierkegaard and Husserl. Even the density of these philosophers' names suggested complex ideas I couldn't begin to keep straight in my head. But Ralph also liked to fool around, and he had a laugh that brought joy to my high school days. We'd play conga drums on our desks during algebra class until we were thrown out and walked down the hill and through a broken fence to a deli on 241st Street, where we ate Devil Dogs or something else delectable and talked about an Antonioni film marveling at the unusual beauty of Monica Vitti. Weekends, my jazz-loving mom smuggled us into the Five Spot to groove on Thelonious Monk, Charles Mingus, or John Coltrane, and then Monday mornings, we were feverishly rapping rhythms on our school desks until our beleaguered math teacher threw us out onto the streets of adolescent bliss.

Whenever I asked Ralph about life with his mom, dad, and sister, who lived a couple of miles away in a dreary two-family house within walking distance of the 242nd Street stop of the 7th Avenue line, my friend shrugged and didn't have much to say. Not that I really cared very much. We went to sexy movies and my mom took us to hear jazz. What did I care about his boring home life?

At the end of junior year, each member of our English class chose a poem to explicate in front of the class. I choose Dylan Thomas's, "The Ballad of the Long-Legged Bait." Though I hadn't actually read the poem, at a glance I noticed references to fishing that made it an easy choice for me. My dad had been taking me fishing since I was a young boy, and I had a knack for hooking eels in the Long Island Sound. But I was nervous to be speaking in front of the whole class, and our teacher, Charles Ellis, was a man I greatly admired.

About midnight before my talk, I sat down to read the poem.

She longs among horses and angels,
The rainbow-fish bend in her joys,
Floated the lost cathedral
Chimes of the rocked buoys.

I read it and read it. I didn't have a clue. There were a few fish but no fishing that I could see. I couldn't figure out what was going on.

The whirled boat in the burn of his blood
Is crying from nets to knives,
Oh the shearwater birds and their boatsized brood
Oh the bulls of Biscay and their calves . . .

I was sweating, couldn't think of a sentence to say about Thomas's masterpiece. What would I do? In my fantasy, Charles Ellis was going to be my guide and gateway to literary fame. But if I couldn't even explain a simple fish poem, Ellis would know that I was a fraud. Maybe I was a fraud.

The whirled boat in the burn of his blood
Is crying from nets to knives . . .

What the hell was Dylan Thomas talking about?
At one in the morning, I phoned Ralph. He didn't mind

late calls, and we often spoke long into the night. Ralph read the poem quickly and explained that mutability is often at the heart of great poems; and then taking a cue from my silence, he added, "Kid, that means that nothing good ever lasts." While I mulled this over, Ralph quoted a line from another Dylan Thomas poem, "I see the boys of summer in their ruin." "Do you get it kid? We are marked by death in the flower of our youth." Amazing. Immediately, I was taken with this idea. Then he read another line from the poem. "Let us summon Death from a summer woman," The notion of mutability for me at sixteen was love at first sight. It seemed so fucking cool. Ralph explained a few other stanzas of the fish poem and said that basically it was an allegory on death and salvation that takes place in a fishing boat.

The next morning in English class, I gave an oral report on mutability in Dylan Thomas's poetry. I used all the ideas Ralph had told me several hours earlier. Some of what I said I didn't understand, but Ralph was so confident I never doubted him. Everyone thought my talk was amazing.

I closed with these lines:

And the fisherman winds his reel
With no more desire than a ghost.

I heard one of the other boys whispering. "How did Fred know all of that?"

Mutability was so fucking cool.

~

Although Ralph was my best friend, I didn't feel great affection or tenderness for him, at least not in a normal sense. I couldn't imagine giving Ralph a hug after scoring the winning shot in a basketball game because he didn't know how to play basketball. He wasn't interested in football, stickball, or fishing, not interested in making money like my dad. When I tried to reach out to him, I could never take hold, not really. We weren't on the same page, sometimes close, but never the same page, and I never knew exactly what page Ralph was on. Somehow, we operated in a middle ground. Ralph spoke about his ideas as if he were translating from a different language so I could understand.

~

After college when Ralph moved out of the city, there were long gaps of time between phone calls. It was that way with a lot of friends from high school and college where friendship felt eternal until time passed and even to recall the names of once cherished soulmates became hard.

Ralph's occasional calls would begin the same way: "How you doin', kid?" he'd ask, this absurd salutation exactly the same as in high school when he'd call from his parents' place to discuss what foreign film we'd sneak in to see Saturday night or where we'd go for Chinese food.

"How you doin', kid?" I have answered in kind for decades,

but during one of these calls, my question had taken on an absurdity that cracked us both up. Ralph was now living in Florida but no longer had a fixed address. For a couple of months, he'd been sleeping at a distant cousin's, but after that he camped out on a park bench not far from the Fontainebleau hotel, where my salesman dad had taken me a couple of times on vacation when he was flush from a big lighting-fixture sale.

My friend Ralph was trying on the homeless dream I'd shared with him during our high school days that I'd been too conventional or fearful to try myself. Ralph was slumming for a while in the manner of George Orwell who'd written about living the street life in London, Henry Miller who had been homeless in Paris in the '30s, and Jack Kerouac, of course, who had made the street life famous.

When I graduated from college, I thought about living on the street to see how it would feel and where it would lead me as a writer. But I never had the courage to give it a real try. I hitchhiked to New York from Ohio two or three times. And I half-assed it a couple of warm summer nights when I was in graduate school at NYU. I nervously walked from my apartment in the Village and tried to get comfortable on a bench in Washington Square Park, attempted to doze off while terrified I'd be knifed to death trolling for literary treasure. Then I ran home at dawn to write pretentious notes about how it felt to be hungry and homeless in a park.

"How you doin', kid?"

"Fine, I suppose," Ralph chuckled, then asked politely about the kids and my work. I was gracious, as I recall, but feeling a little annoyed as writers sometimes do when a friend has edged closer to material he had planned to write about himself.

I could tell that Ralph was impatient to describe his newest ideas for inventions, for getting rich. "What have you been into?" I asked.

"I've been thinking a lot," he said. For many years, Ralph has been thinking about things I knew little about.

Then, speaking with executive crispness, he talked about an invention, a computer program for business management he had been designing in his head. Then he told me about an idea he was refining in modal logic. I don't have the mind for modal logic. Almost no one does.

~

But Ralph didn't seem to notice, and as he dipped further into the language of analytic philosophy, I swallowed my annoyance and found myself recalling starry nights I'd spent decades earlier, beside the shimmering pool at the Fontainebleau hotel just down the block from where my old friend was talking in a phone booth. While my father sipped a scotch and described to me his latest commercial lighting deal, I watched women shake and slither to the licentious rhythms of a poolside rhumba band. I recalled one night watching Xavier Cugat and Abbe Lane perform in the nightclub. What a beat on the congas as Abbe Lane swung her hips! There was just too much greatness in Miami Beach to take in. There was greyhound racing, jai lai, and Wolfie's delicatessen nearby for the best corned beef and chopped chicken liver, sport fishing boats lined up at the dock for high seas adventure in waters Hemingway had trolled for marlin. And just outside the glistening hotel, there were shining, sweet-smelling convertibles pulling up to the massive golden doors, beautiful women stepping out of these cars, entering that cathedral of pleasure. Miami Beach was a tidal wave of erotic promise.

~

More than fifty years have now passed since the Five Spot, Coltrane, Monk, and Mingus have left us. My mom is long gone. So many whom I have loved are gone. Wolfie's is gone. There are no more marlins off Miami Beach, yet the Fontainebleau remains. Somehow it persists. When I occasionally visit Miami Beach, I check it out, walk inside the enormous lobby, hoping for the rush of grandeur I felt as a boy. But the great lobby needs a paint job, bellhops now wear shabby outfits, soggy towels smelling of chlorine are bunched in clumps alongside the aged pool. Still, I feel a vestige of splendor standing in the lobby. I think of my dad looking up at the gigantic chandelier and saying, "Wow," with his chin quivering a little. It really is a magnificent lighting fixture.

There was so much that I misperceived about my friend Ralph. From our occasional phone calls over the decades, I retained a few lines that had grown crusty with time, hung on to them like lyrics from songs long ago grown stale.

"How you doin', kid?" A laugh or two. "How you doin', kid?"

I no longer had time for my old buddy. I wanted to get off the phone after a half minute and only barely listened to his notions. I could hardly think of another word to say to him. I was raising a family. I was busy looking for stories to write for magazines. I had become a beggar for stories. I would chat up total strangers in the subway or in a bar or restaurant or even in an elevator wondering if they had an interesting story to tell me. And I was busy thinking about pro football. Going fishing. Missing my father. Worrying about getting older. There was so much to do. I just wasn't interested anymore in Ralph. Maybe I had never been. It was hard to remember who we once were.

But one afternoon, I called him from New York. For some reason, I felt ready to hear his story, maybe because I had recently lost three close friends. I hadn't spoken with Ralph in two years. I wasn't even sure he was still alive. The first of many mornings on the phone, Ralph couldn't remember long gaps of time, even years. I asked him to try. He would recall one or two things and then he'd go blank. "I can't remember," he'd say impatiently, "Ask me something else." When I pressed him, he sounded annoyed, and I thought he would give up.

Then after more sputtering exchanges, his whole life tumbled out in revelations I could never have imagined.

Part II

In the years before I knew Ralph in high school, he lived with his parents and older sister in a small two-family house a few blocks from us in the Bronx. His father Isaac was a Jewish emigrant from Israel, a short, powerfully built man with a heavy accent who operated a small textile business out of a lower Manhattan loft. Isaac had the singular ambition to become wealthy in his new country. He would do whatever it took to succeed—anything at all. Ralph's mom Sadie kept a kosher home and lived anxious days bridled with superstitions and malaise. She worried about what color socks her husband should wear each morning to the factory, precisely the time he should leave for work, not ten minutes later or earlier, whether to serve lamb chops on Wednesday or Sunday. In her view, such decisions were key to Isaac's success and the prosperity and happiness of her family. Sadie was unflappable about her beliefs and her ability to intuit the future. Everyone in the family made fun of Sadie's ways, but they listened to her as her prophesies were more than occasionally on the mark.

In the third grade, Ralph still wasn't reading. He didn't play sports with other kids. He didn't make friends. He sometimes seemed to be chatting or fervently arguing with himself. These dialogues made others in the family uncomfortable, and he was badgered to stop. This confused Ralph, and he tried to keep his conversations private.

"I was faking it a lot of the time, not just with you, but with everyone. My whole life, people around me have seemed to know things I didn't know about. I was always missing the point.

"Seemed like everyone had social knowledge I didn't share," he told me. "They were playing some sort of game I couldn't understand. People edging for different types of advantage by signaling to one another in ways I didn't understand. Often it felt like a sadistic game. But I learned to smile and agree. I learned to fake it."

~

Ralph's sister Ann was a stocky girl with a lovely face. She was the smartest member of the family, an excellent student, an attacking chess player as a child and later on a star on the City College chess team. Ann was a protégée of her father, whom she adored. She was fearless, and before she matured, she'd rough-house with boys on the street. She was protective of her younger brother. One day, she was studying chess on the porch of their house when a couple of older kids pushed Ralph to the ground on the sidewalk.

While they laughed and called him weird, Ralph looked more perplexed than hurt, but Ann ran down the steps and began flailing at the boys. One of them grabbed her arms while the other hit her in the face and belly. Their blows increased her rage. She threatened and kicked back at the one holding her, dared the other one to hit her again. She called him a pussy. Ralph watched this beating in paralysis and confusion. Fighting was outside his orbit like stickball or hoops. The boy smacked her around while she cursed spitting blood. Finally, in confusion at this raging girl, the boy let her go. Ann turned and kicked him in the balls. She screamed they were sissies for running away. "I'll kill you if you ever come back here again." If she had a gun, they would have been dead on the street.

Twelve-year-old Ann worried what would become of her brother who kept his own counsel and sometimes seemed to chat with birds landed on his windowsill. She decided he must be retarded. She discussed Ralph with her mom. What to do about their unusual boy who couldn't read and had invisible friends.

Then one day at the end of fourth grade, Ralph picked up a book and began reading aloud. No one in the family nor his teachers in school could understand how this was possible, that overnight, this boy who did not read a single word could suddenly read fluently. But to Ralph, this didn't seem surprising. There was so much Ralph didn't understand. He felt like he was from another planet. He told me when we were in high school that he was an alien. He had a funny way of putting things—an alien. We both grinned at the idea of it. I loved that. My friend the alien. Ralph the alien. To speak to people, his family, friends in school, teachers, he told me, he needed to stretch himself, as if learning to speak another language, their language, relate to their passions that he didn't share or understand, so he could pass. I thought this was incredibly cool. My friend was offbeat like Charlie Mingus and Thelonious Monk. That's why he could relate so easily to their music. I decided that Jack Kerouac would have loved to have known Ralph.

~

Before Ralph and I finished high school, Isaac had left the textile business for real-estate and had cultivated union and mob connections, including a partnership on many deals with Sammy "The Bull" Gravano. With the help of his new friend who understood the nuances of threats and bribes, Isaac managed to broker an office building deal involving the legendary developer William Zeckendorf. Isaac arranged the sale of a hotel in the Bronx and suddenly the family had money; they moved from their small, rented house near the subway to a spacious home in Riverdale overlooking the Hudson.

Isaac was the family hero, but Ralph didn't know what to make of him. Isaac was a physically strong man with a crude, threatening manner. In business he played by different rules or no rules at all. Isaac would kill if that was what it took to win big. Ralph felt this even as a kid. He was more like his mom who was guided through difficult times by intuitions. Sadie's intuitions were born out in profits.

~

Isaac's real estate business and the life changes it afforded became the guiding light in their family. Everything else was much less important. Isaac and Sadie ran the show in tandem, strange though that might seem. Isaac made the connections, made the payoffs, closed the deals, handled the money. Sadie said yes or no, when to make a sale, when to let it pass. Isaac railed against the insanity of his wife's superstitions and predictions, but in the end he listened to her. He came to believe that her prophesies were key to their success.

They all listened to her. Nearly everything in their lives seemed to hang on Sadie's predictions. When mother and son went to S. Klein's to buy Ralph trousers, she took his hand off a pair of corduroys he'd selected and said fearfully, "Not this one, Ralph." She had knowledge something terrible would happen to him if they bought this pair of pants. Ralph was afraid to cross her. Sadie would foresee secrets of the universe by the hour. There was always some reason, some spiritual reason, or some Jewish reason that only Sadie could divine.

When Ralph was still in elementary school, Sadie bought him a parakeet. Each day when he came home from school, the bird would fly down the stairs from Ralph's small bedroom and land on his shoulder. The parakeet was always happy to see Ralph. It never visited anyone else in the family. They had become friends. Ralph would sit in a hard-backed chair in the corner of the living room, and they would chat for an hour or two until Isaac came home and harshly brushed the bird from his son's shoulder. It made Isaac uncomfortable that Ralph talked to a bird. Even Sadie was troubled that her son had unusual habits and his own intuitions she couldn't understand. Ralph's friendship with the parakeet turned out to be even more troubling to the family than the long conversations Ralph had been having with himself.

One day Ralph came home from school and the bird was gone. "Flew right out the window," was what Sadie explained. Ralph was horrified. They think they can cure me by killing my bird, he reasoned, having difficulty even looking at his mother who had been his lifeline. He knew in his bones one of them had put his bird in the garbage.

For Isaac, Sadie, and Ann, the family business was their fortress. On all critical matters they believed they needed to hang together. Otherwise, Dad's business would get swept away, and they'd all be swept away with it. Ralph was the weak link. He spent time talking with a bird. Any one of them might have helped the bird disappear, even Ann who adored her brother. They believed Ralph needed to toughen up to survive in the world.

But the business prospered. Isaac bought a twenty-eight-story office building on Broadway and enlisted the Gravano crew to demo the interior and build new offices. By now, Sammy "The Bull" Gravano had temporarily given up crime for a dry wall construction and pool installation business that was making big money. Soon, Isaac leveraged the Broadway building to purchase a large factory space in White Plains, renovated it with his new friend, and rented it to IBM for their world headquarters. Sadie continued to play her part: "Buy it today, Isaac," "Not this one," "Not this month," or "Not this deal, Isaac." Each time she stopped him from making a deal, Isaac stormed the kitchen raging, "Why not?" "Are you crazy? They are giving away money." but always he relented. Surely, Sadie was crazy, but her intuitions were uncanny. She could sense a good deal like a prophet. They all had a role. Ann was a brilliant student, an ardent fan of early Mick Jagger, a precocious reader of literary classics. Yet, she backed Isaac no matter what he said or did, no matter how coarse or wayward, or unsavory his partners. She didn't even care about his mistresses, decided they were useful. They made him feel young. Sadie agreed. "So what?" No matter about his shady business partners. "Who cares?" They all remembered poverty. Now they were killing it.

~

But by the time we were in our senior year of high school, Ralph felt suffocated by his Jewish neighborhood and the mercenary obsessions of his family. Many in our prep school went to Ivy League colleges, but Ralph didn't believe he could survive a month at Princeton, Yale, or Columbia. Also, he wanted to get further away from his family. He applied to the University of Wisconsin.

Freshman year he enrolled in a junior college within the university offering less-challenging courses for weaker students. Even here, Ralph didn't think he'd last a month. But predictably, the courses were easy for him, and he enjoyed the company of pretty eighteen-year-old girls from the Midwest.

During his sophomore year, he met Jean, a short rather plain-looking girl with a taste for beautiful shoes and scarves, French wines and cheeses. She was a classics major, fluent in German and French, and, remarkably, Jean also had refined knowledge of ancient Greek and Egyptian. The first time they went to a museum together, Jean fluently translated for Ralph from ancient Egyptian. This absolutely blew his mind.

Jean was wary of men but had a special affinity for dogs and cats. "From the start, she thought of me as a pet," Ralph told me. "I guess we were both like pets. A lot of our communication was expressions and sidelong glances, unspoken ironies, and small delights, sounds we made up. We had a cat and sometimes we pretended we were cats. We developed a private language, a secret way to communicate."

They became intimate in the manner of two pets. They had running jokes that did not involve talking. They established a common understanding about people that was conveyed in a nod or a grin. They would thrill each other wordlessly. Gestures and hints were their language. "I became like a panther to her, a big cat. Because in her view, I had certain strength. I didn't understand this, but it was moving to me. I thought it was cool."

People were drawn to Jean, especially other eccentrics and academic stars at Wisconsin. In her unspoken manner, she became a facilitator for Ralph. Shortly after they began living together, Ralph formed a friendship with the editor of the literary magazine and before long was introduced to another acquaintance of Jean's,

David Unger, a brilliant associate professor of philosophy, a rising star in the field of epistemology.

For the first two years at Wisconsin, Ralph wandered from course to course, composing poetry in his head, studying economics, literature. "I didn't really have a solid understanding of what I was doing—it was all sort of instinctive and reactive. My ideas were very abstract. A professor counseled I'd never make a living in economics and suggested that I should study philosophy."

Okay, he'd study philosophy. Why not?

~

Back home in the Bronx, Ralph's sister had now married Sherman, an unattractive, overweight man who didn't know the difference between Jane Austen and Spiderman, but he knew the building business and was a cutthroat negotiator. We needed Sherman to save the business, Sadie told Ralph during a visit home from college. Sadie understood her husband's limitations. By now Isaac owned too much real estate to keep track of himself. There weren't hours enough in the day. Ralph's parents urged their daughter to make the marriage and she obliged. "I guess it was like being in a gangster family," Ralph reflected more than fifty years later. "It was like being a good soldier. It was the price you pay."

One evening before Ralph returned to school, Ann and her brother went to a film in Manhattan, and coming out of the theater, Ann noticed a little sports car parked along the sidewalk. She was struck by the unusual beauty of the car, a green Morgan, which seemed like a living creature. For Ann, the Morgan embodied the adventure and mystery of a life she would never have a chance to know. She told Ralph she would love to have a car like this, and her brother answered that Sadie, Isaac, and Sherman wouldn't feel comfortable about her driving such a car. It was too weird and impractical. Also, it was a standard shift car and Ann didn't know how to drive a standard shift.

~

Philosophy came easily to Ralph although his ideas were usually off the beaten track. One day, in a course on Aristotle and Plato, he delivered a paper on a Socratic dialogue written in the fourth century BCE by Plato called "Philebus," which discusses in part the life of physical pleasures versus the life of pleasures of the mind. Most students in the class weren't terribly interested in Ralph's unusual take on the dialogue nor was the professor teaching the course. But one student who was dressed like a disheveled janitor came up to Ralph after class and speaking in a thick Yiddish accent launched into his analysis of Ralph's offbeat interpretation. Bob Weingard was enthralled by Ralph's paper, and they left the class talking ardently.

Ralph and Weingard—Ralph always called him "Weingard"—walked about a mile to a rented ramshackle house near railroad tracks Weingard shared with three other students, all the while talking about Plato, Socratic dialogues, and physics, Weingard's true passion about which Ralph knew little. Inside,

Ralph was hit with the smell of rotting food and old marijuana. The sparse furniture was old and broken, and in a corner there was a contraption that looked like the back end of a refrigerator, some kind of machine that the students were using for making mescaline.

This was the first day of Ralph's thirty-year friendship with Bob Weingard. They bonded like kindred spirits. Weingard was drawn to Ralph's mind and didn't care much about the rest of his life. For him, philosophy was life. For many of the ensuing years, Ralph and Weingard tested ideas about philosophy against each other, a back and forth that sometimes yielded bold, original ideas. From time to time, Ralph was cited in papers written by Weingard or by his major professor at Wisconsin, David Unger.

∽

When Ralph returned to New York the summer following his junior year, he was surprised to find that his sister was eight months pregnant, and most afternoons she spent cruising around Riverdale and Westchester in a green Morgan convertible. Ralph had never seen Ann more happy than tooling around in that little car with the top down, her hair blowing in the wind, The Rolling Stones crackling from the small car radio. Ralph fancied that while she drove, his sister was daydreaming about other paths she might have taken.

∽

Ralph left Wisconsin before finishing his Ph.D. The formality of a degree didn't interest him, and he was bored with school life. He decided he could best develop as a philosopher studying on his own, occasionally conferring with David Unger but mainly with Weingard, who was now teaching at Rutgers.

Like a normal affluent couple, Ralph and Jean rented a lovely three-bedroom apartment on York Avenue that Jean filled with Persian carpets and tasteful antiques. She wore a little apron when she cooked her savory French cuisine. They bought a new Saab for monthly drives to Vermont where her family lived. In the spring, they purchased a twenty-eight-foot sloop, which they kept at a marina on City Island, taught themselves how to sail, and enjoyed weekend cruises on the Long Island Sound. There was plenty of money from Isaac's business for anything they might want. They ate in fine restaurants and created a small wine cellar featuring Jean's favorite French wines. Ralph occasionally stopped by Isaac's office and wrote a few business letters for Isaac when he was asked. But for the most part, he was oblivious to his father's tactics and associations.

However, his sister's unhappiness was hard to avoid. Ann had married Sherman for the future of her family, for the business. But Sherman disgusted her. He had no interest in books or paintings or music. He slurped his food. He smelled of sweat and avarice. She hated it when he touched her, but he required sex nearly each day. He was forcing her to make a baby each year. The babies were a sea anchor affirming the long future of their wholly disagreeable relationship.

When Ralph and Jean returned from Wisconsin to live in the city, Ann was no longer driving her Morgan. After a trip to Tennessee with her baby, Ann was distraught to find the green Morgan no longer parked in the driveway of the large Riverdale house where the family lived. Sherman hated that car from day one. More than hated it. His wife's afternoon sojourns in the Morgan were a statement of her independence and, more still, of her yearning for an independent future.

When Ann came home from Tennessee, Sadie told her daughter that the car had been stolen from their driveway; it was gone and that was that. Then with a knowing expression that had the weight of a biblical judgment, Sadie suggested, maybe it was better that the Morgan was gone, a sign we shouldn't own such a car.

"Sherman made it go away," Ann bitterly told her brother. "They do that all the time. My father and Sherman, they make things disappear."

~

Ralph was mainly alone now in his apartment on York Avenue, studying philosophy as Jean was away four or five days a week and occasionally for longer stretches of time, finishing her Ph.D at the University of Pennsylvania. Ralph was so entrenched in ideas her absences were barely noticed. Once or twice a month, he came to his dad's office for a change of scenery and occasionally he traveled to New Jersey to confer with visiting philosophers at Rutgers and with Weingard, who was making a reputation in philosophy of physics and quantum mechanics.

One afternoon the two friends met at Rockefeller University on the east side of Manhattan to hear a lecture by Saul Kripke on modal logic. Lectures by Kripke were star-studded events in philosophy, and the audience that night was filled with top academic philosophers from all over the country, including several Nobel laureates. Kripke was a true genius. He had read all of Shakespeare's work in the fourth grade and started teaching himself geometry and calculus in the last year of grammar school. At the time of the Rockefeller lecture, he was widely considered one of the two or three most important philosophers of the twentieth century, on a par with Bertrand Russell.

Following Kripke's dazzling but extremely esoteric talk, guests including Weingard and Ralph were invited to have dinner in the elegant Rockefeller dining room. Kripke was seated at the head of their table. At one point he stood up as if remembering something and walked over to Ralph whom he recognized from a talk months earlier at one of the New Jersey Colleges.

Kripke wanted to know if Ralph had made progress in the work he had been doing on the liar's paradox, and Ralph nodded yes. They began trading ideas about the liar's paradox. When Ralph needed to leave for home, Kripke surprised his dinner guests by following Ralph out of the dining room. The two men took a bus uptown to Ralph's apartment where they continued for hours debating Ralph's idea of a way to decompose the paradox to make it a simple contradiction.

Kripke was, in fact, more interested in a complex contemporary paradox called Russell's paradox that he'd been working on for some time. Ralph had been unable to generalize what he'd discovered so it would apply to Russell's paradox, but using Ralph's approach, Kripke made a fabulous discovery.

~

Sammy "The Bull" Gravano made his reputation as underboss of the Gambino crime family. In 1992, when Gravano opted to turn state's evidence against John Gotti and other mob luminaries, Gravano confessed to nineteen murders, implicating Gotti in four of them. Less known is that Gravano had also amassed a fortune from more pacific business enterprises. By 1998, his construction and pool business had branched into lucrative concrete paving, and he was making millions. "I literally controlled Manhattan, literally," he commented.

But in the 1970s, when Sammy Gravano was starting out in the construction business, Ralph's father had used him primarily to demo the interiors of his newly purchased office buildings and factory spaces. Also, Isaac had introduced Gravano to favorite politicians on the take, and Sammy repaid Isaac in various ways.

The afternoon that Ralph met Gravano in Isaac's office, Ralph only had spotty knowledge about the background of his father's partner. Gravano and Ralph had an affable talk for about an hour. Ralph's impression was that Sammy Gravano was a friendly man, intelligent and well spoken, despite his violent reputation. Ralph was open to the idea that people change and found it amusing that Sammy "The Bull" was his dad's business partner.

As Ralph had grown older and less rudderless, Isaac became more open with his son, even harboring hope that someday Ralph would be able to take over his growing real estate operation. Naturally he wanted to pass on the secrets of his success to Ralph. "The business is our bank," Isaac said more than once and each time with solemnity. "You're smart, Ralph. Don't be so shy. . . . Come into the office a few days a week, introduce yourself to our suppliers." Ralph looked up from his books, smiled a little and nodded thoughtfully whenever his dad made life suggestions. Unless he was doing philosophy, Ralph was not an argumentative man.

For years now, Isaac had been making a fortune stealing from his own business. "You offer them the account if they give you five thousand cash." When Isaac said such things, Ralph would laugh and change the subject. His reluctance annoyed the hell out of Isaac as it had once infuriated him that his son enjoyed talking to birds. "What's wrong with you, Ralph? Grow up a little." Isaac became red in the face talking reason to his son who was so refined and talented at reasoning. There were often suppliers stopping by the office, electrical contractors, electricians, lighting salesmen, suppliers of heating oil, AC suppliers, plumbers, exterminators, garbage collectors, and many more. Kickbacks were Isaac's money tree. Isaac had taught Sherman how to do it, and Sherman was pulling in a fortune on side deals—much more than he earned in salary. Isaac encouraged Ann as well because she also came into the office. Why not? Why not? Tax-free money. Kickbacks were Isaac's way of life and he wanted to share this gift with his children. But like her brother, Ann also couldn't steal from the business. For her, this was a step too far.

One day Ralph happened to be studying philosophy in Isaac's office when a lady walked through the door trailing four children. She was a Marilyn knockoff, blond, busty, and wearing a revealing low-cut blouse and short skirt. She moved around the office as if she'd been here before, shuffled through a few things on Isaac's desk, opened one of his drawers looking around for something. Shook her head, disgusted. The kids went to a far corner of the office, opened the drawer of a filling cabinet, pulled out some toys, and began playing on the floor. The lady sat in a chair, folding her shapely legs. She commanded the room, seemed not to notice Ralph at all, and then for a moment she looked through him like hired help. Isaac wouldn't be back for an hour or two, Ralph offered shyly. A few hours?! She was annoyed, muttered something. She seemed to own the place. Said she'd take the kids to lunch and ordered Ralph to tell Isaac she'd be back and to find the Blue Cross Blue Shield cards—she needed them today!

Ralph asked her name, and she seemed affronted as if a hired lacky had crossed a line. Her name was Shelley Silverman. What? What did you say? This name echoed in Ralph's head. Shelley Silverman? Trying to make sense. Who was Shelley Silverman? "Who are you?" he managed.

"I'm here to see my husband," she said like a queen. "Who are you?"

"I'm Ralph." He could not think of another word to say.

~

On the surface, the news of Isaac's bigamy changed very little in the Silverman house. Parked outside in the driveway were three homely Studebaker Lark sedans for Ann, Sherman, and Sadie, gifts to Isaac from an electrical contractor he'd recently brought on to handle two older buildings being renovated by Sammy Gravano. In the kitchen, Sadie's chicken and unfertilized chicken eggs simmered in chicken fat. Sadie and Ann seemed to have absorbed the astonishing news into the habits of their lives. Sadie advised her husband to buy another older building on West 28th Street, and Isaac ridiculed her fortune-telling but went ahead and closed the deal. Ann tended to her four young children, tried to avoid Sherman's ardor whenever possible. She adored her father and would stand by him whatever he did, whatever he needed to do. The family was swimming in money—more than enough for all their whims and dreams. By sharing the truth with his family, Isaac had freed himself to spend half his nights with his other family at their estate in Rye, New York. Isaac had pulled off his own American dream. "If this is what Isaac needs," Sadie and Ann said to each other.

If that's what Isaac needed, the Silvermans all believed it, including Ralph, who was preoccupied with new ideas, as always. Given a little time to adjust, my friend could accept most things. But I couldn't believe it when Ralph told me. I thought he had made up the whole crazy tale. I begged him to take me to see Isaac's other home.

One summer afternoon Ralph and I drove up to Rye in one of the family Larks because Jean had taken the Saab away to school. My friend wasn't especially interested in this visit except to please me. He was anxious to tell me about the research he was doing in computer programming, but I had little patience to listen. I was jumping out of my skin to see the trappings of his father's second life.

Isaac's twelve-acre property was luscious, green rolling lawns with specimen trees, tailored gardens filled with curated plantings, and two greenhouses for vegetables and exotic flowers. As we idled toward the large house, I could see the Long Island Sound to our right through a grove of tall spruce and elm trees. We parked Sadie's Lark in a long, circular driveway beside two shiny BMWs and walked to the house. Ralph told me his dad had purchased the property several years earlier from the estate of the actor Errol Flynn. Yes, that Errol Flynn. Isaac had gotten a deal because the house and guest house had been empty and badly neglected for more than twenty years since the actor's death.

When we walked into the spacious living room, Shelley Silverman barely acknowledged us, which was jarring and quickened the pace of our tour. The sprawling sixteen-room house was high ceilinged with Venetian plaster walls, copper skylights, a custom white-marble kitchen. The place was gorgeous. I wanted to linger to see more, but Ralph was nervous within earshot of his second mother who had nothing to say to him. For some reason she seemed to hold my brilliant friend in contempt.

The high point of the day for me was the swimming pool. I had never seen a pool like this one installed by Sammy Gravano.

Not even the fantastic pool at the Miami Beach Fontainebleau, which had lodged in my memory for years, held a candle to Isaac's huge pool bordered by terra-cotta tiles and blooming hydrangeas. There was a built-in island on one end offering a surface to rest drinks or lie out in the sunshine. Behind the island end of the pool was a large hot tub and three posh enclosed cabanas designed for pleasure. But what jumped out at me was the rich mysterious navy blue pool water, as if it had been imported from the Gulf Stream. How could pool water look like this? It called to me to dive in, but my friend was jumping out of his skin. His new mother was laying nearby on a pool chair turning through a glamor magazine. Shelley had Ralph completely unnerved.

Isaac was asleep in another pool chair, his arms, legs, and big belly matted in body hair with tanning oil. He was bald, his neck folding into his chin. Shelley stood up holding a mixed drink, walked past her husband, and then past us without a glance. Ralph's dad was old, ugly, and coarse. I wondered if she liked him even a little. Did money matter this much? Did this this palace matter so much? I wondered if she ever kissed him on the mouth? I wondered if she ever thought about his other family, their ambitions, their habits, their sorrows? Did she consider his other life at all? Or where the money for all of this came from? She was surely beautiful. Sexy. Very sexy. A memorable walk. But could she please him month after year? Would she?

When I counted now, there were five children, not four, playing around the pool. She had her hands filled with five kids. I wondered if she was a good mother. Two of them seemed to have

Isaac's nose. The others had Nordic features. Was there another Isaac before Isaac? Would there be another Isaac after Isaac? My friend Ralph had no idea which of the children were his siblings. He would be too shy to ask such a question. But he didn't really care. He cared greatly about other things she and Isaac would never know or care about. But was the splendid world Isaac had fashioned here enough to hold his interest; the gardens, the dark-tiled hot tub, the sound of wind through the trees? Her voluptuous body? Probably. Maybe. Someday will he need to move on to another younger woman, another estate?

Ralph couldn't restrain himself, giggled a little at the absurdity of it all. I loved him for that. I wondered about the previous owner of this place. How could I not? Isaac was now walking in Errol Flynn's footsteps. Did this please him? But probably he didn't realize half of it? Errol Flynn had brought dozens of mistresses to visit this sumptuous property, had sailed with each of them in the afternoon on his yacht *Sirocco*, an appetizer for the voluptuous evening ahead. Errol Flynn's seventy-three-foot yacht was moored in the sound within view of the house when the trees had been less profuse. He had enjoyed Ava Gardner on this property, also Jean Harlow, Anita Ekberg, Lana Turner. There were many others. There had been so many silky afternoons of pleasure beside a pool far more modest than this one, times that felt like they could never end for Errol Flynn just as this afternoon surely felt eternal for Isaac Silverman.

But did it? Almost surely, this was my fantasy, but not Isaac's, who kept his eye on the real estate market even on long weekends out of the city, always looking for a good deal on an old building.

I would have liked to stay longer, to watch the evening shadows fall onto the majestic property, to see night-lights flickering on the Long Island Sound. But not Ralph. I could feel he was edgy to get back to the city. He was working with a new personal computer on a project that had possessed his imagination.

~

Sherman leached most of Ann out of Ann with compulsive talk of schemes and payoffs, mothering his four babies, miles of laundry, years of distasteful fucking, and the smell of his rank body. She could barely remember intellectual or aesthetic pleasures, occasionally wondered if such delicacies were ever retrievable. I knew her briefly when she was in college. Ann's yearnings were captivating. I once had dreams of making her my girl, but she was older than I was, way smarter, and too sophisticated. I couldn't imagine Ann now as Ralph described her to me. Like a spent swimmer grasping a sinking lifeboat, she held on to her man, her father, whatever he needed to do, whatever he decided was necessary to save the family. This had always been the law of the family. Whatever was necessary.

It's hard to say what happened next or whose fault it was. Sadie was becoming petulant and making poor decisions, that's what he claimed. Or perhaps it was Isaac who was losing his touch. Sadie had warned her husband about buying the 28th Street building, but Isaac had gone ahead and made the deal, then dolled up the offices. Afterward, the offices had remained empty. Customers weren't even stopping by to take a look.

But when the massive IBM building was approaching the time for a rent renewal, Sadie argued they should wait until the final sixty days of the lease, then bargain hard for a 10 percent increase. Isaac was reluctant to play hardball but heeded his wife. The day of the fateful meeting with IBM attorneys, Isaac came with a new contract in hand calling for a 10 percent rental increase, which would net the family an additional five hundred thousand dollars a year, but he was stunned to hear that IBM would be vacating the factory space in sixty days at the end of their lease. The family would soon be sitting on 400,000 square feet of empty factory space in White Plains with taxes, insurance, and mortgage payments each month.

In fairness to both Isaac and Sadie, the real estate market in Manhattan was changing by the day with scores of shiny new office buildings climbing into the Manhattan skyline. The Twin Towers was nearing completion and offering businesses almost 10 million square feet of spectacular office space featuring the best views in Manhattan. Tenants were no longer very interested in fifty-year-old buildings with broken boilers and littered elevators that frequently didn't work.

～

Despair and foreboding can sometimes be the gateway to a creative tsunami. As the family business faltered, Ralph became flooded with ideas. Ideas for get-rich inventions came into his head as if Thomas Edison were whispering to him. In his sleep, he dreamed of memory circuits and of an engine operated by magnets. He tried to work out the mathematics of his engine that wouldn't need fuel, but that turned out to be a dead end. He envisioned a gas tank that would have a built-in fire retardant so that a crashed car wouldn't burn up or explode. He patented this idea. A couple of companies were interested, but he was never able to make a deal. Dead ends hardly mattered to my friend. New ideas for inventions came to him like poetry had once jumped into his head in Wisconsin or new breakthroughs in philosophy that continued to intrigue Saul Kripke during his lunches with Ralph in Manhattan.

In the 1970s, my friend believed computers would change the world. Someday these machines would be able to do things we could not imagine, he told a small group of us one night. He predicted that computers would learn to have sentient abilities— someday they would function like people.

"I'm interested in sorting and searching," he went on to explain. "What if I gave you a large box with five thousand index cards in random order. How long would it take you to sort these cards if your life depended on getting it perfectly correct, cross-checking all the cards so there wouldn't be one tiny mistake. How long would it take you? A week? Two weeks? Longer? A couple of months ago, when I first bought my new computer, I could do the job in three minutes. But working on the machine for several weeks, reprograming it, I found a way to make the computer much faster. The software that I improved could be the gateway to applications I can't even dream of."

Ralph's confidence discussing his inventions, technology, and philosophy was disconcerting as if he were witnessing a different world than we knew about. Or he understood things we couldn't imagine. Or he was crazy.

Ideas appeared in his dreams, on the subway, or during a phone conversation. Ralph became fixated on digital circuits. He learned how to make his own circuits using something called TTLs, which are a kind of computer chip, a 1970s-style computer chip. Ralph sensed a relationship between these networks of computers and logical functions he discussed with Saul Kripke and Bob Weingard. His idea was that computers would greatly facilitate the work he was doing in philosophy.

He got more TTLs and a board. He wasn't sure yet where this was headed, but he wanted to experiment with these things. Over time, he was able to build a circuit that would divide frequencies into different registers. He was being pulled in this direction but not sure what it might lead to. He was able to build a circuit that would divide frequencies into lower and higher frequencies. He wanted to see what kind of sound it made so he put it through a speaker. He was utterly dumbfounded by the result. It was a kind of music, a buzzy version of "Hare Krishna." Just like guys chant in Washington Square Park.

One night, five or six of us went to Ralph's apartment and he played this strange synthetic music. We all listened for an hour or so. It was weird and pleasant but didn't seem like much until we tried to stand up and realized we were rocking stoned as if we'd smoked weed or hash. Ralph kept working on his rhythms and tones to make them more harmonious. This was the birth of what he called Pythagoron.

~

Every night at dinner in Riverdale was the same sorry story. The buildings were draining tenants like old leaking ships. Empty buildings were emptying the company accounts. Each night, Sadie urged him, "Sell them, Isaac. Get what you can."

One day, a buyer showed up at Isaac's office and offered him 3 million dollars for his entire business, for all twelve buildings. Sadie begged Isaac to sell, but he laughed at her—that poor lady who had guided him to so many victories. She was convinced the new wife was corrupting his true merchant's heart. Why else wouldn't he listen? He had always listened.

Rebuke settled permanently on Sadie's face: rebuke in the middle of the night when they passed each other in the hall going to the bathroom, rebuke when she served him chicken.

"Stop, Sadie," he tried to warn her. "Who could eat like this?"

"Wrong, Isaac. Wrong. Sell the buildings while you still have something to sell."

Sadie was partially correct about Shelley. Isaac relished visiting his buildings in the afternoon with Shelley trailing along in one of her skimpy outfits, showing off his bodacious young wife as they walked the shabby halls waving like royalty to the remaining tenants. Isaac needed Shelley to see these buildings that he viewed as monuments to his greatness and frequently asked her to come into the city with him. Not too many men own a dozen office buildings, even old ones.

Nights in Riverdale became a bedlam of name calling. Many nights, unless he was too tired or stressed, he would bolt from the house and drive to Rye.

"Go to her," Sadie shrieked as he raced to the door.

"Sadie is not herself anymore," Isaac complained. Or he'd walk into a room muttering, "Nobody knows like I do."

"We're lost, Isaac," she predicted like Medea. "We're all lost. There's no saving it."

~

I enjoyed bringing friends to hear Ralph's invention and Ralph was pleased to show it off. Everyone was astonished by the hallucinogenic effect of his weird music, although several friends left complaining of a headache. One night I asked him, "Ralph, if a company came to you tomorrow and offered you five million cash for it, would you take it and walk away?"

He laughed at me, shook his head no. "Five million for music that gets you stoned. Get real, Fred."

He was working on Pythagoron day and night, beeps and warbles of the "Hare Krishna" mantra spinning through his head whether awake or dozing. Ralph studied brain waves and made adjustments because he sensed that harmonizing brain waves with the sound would amplify the potency of his music. He rarely slept for hours in a row. Perhaps the mania for this work came from a premonition about his father's business.

~

Jean, a lover of opera and classical music, soon began to hate the sounds of Pythagoron. During weekends back in the city from school, she begged him to turn it off, and sometimes he tried for an hour or so with a pained expression as if he were losing the thread of an insight in philosophy. Then when he flipped it back on, he turned the volume up to compensate for lost time, and Jean ran from the room holding her ears. She couldn't do her schoolwork in their apartment. Even when the sounds were turned off for a few hours, they were buzzing in her head, and she couldn't fall asleep at night. After weeks of this, Jean stopped coming home on weekends.

With Jean out of the picture, Ralph's apartment had become a jumble of electronic equipment and takeout containers with clothing strewn about. She was just away for a visit is what he told us. Probably told himself the same. Ralph frequently considered ideas sitting in an austere wooden chair Jean had selected for him in a dusty antique shop in Vermont, his thinking chair. Her books on ancient Greece remained on their shelves until one weekend she stopped by to get them. He hardly noticed when she closed the door for the last time.

Ralph rarely called Riverdale. He rarely called anyone, just worked on Pythagoron. I thought he'd work on it forever, but I was wrong about that. When he felt it was right, Ralph sold his "get-high music" to a small California-based record company. After several months, his music was on a few radio stations in the city, and it was reviewed in the *New York Times* and *Rolling Stone* magazine. Small reviews to be sure, but in each of them it was acknowledged that the music had a hypnotic effect "like smoking marijuana."

Even with his record in hand, Ralph couldn't let the project go. He kept refining his sounds with a new synthesizer, making it stronger and more compelling. He was stoned on his music day and night.

It was during this period that one afternoon working with his headphones on, he happened to hear the phone ringing and picked it up. It was his father.

"Ralphie," his father said in a strained voice. Isaac hadn't addressed his son this way in many years. "Ralphie, your mom. Sadie got a little sick. Just a cold we thought. Then in two days, she died. Just like that. She died. It's a terrible thing. She's gone, Ralphie. We tried to reach you."

Sometimes at the moment of tragic news, mundane matters keep rolling through the mind. You might feel stricken and guilty for wondering what happened in the ninth inning, or you can't stop the song from running through your head. My friend Ralph couldn't stop thinking about Pythagoron. Every twerp and warble that he could now recite like the haftarah kept traveling through his brain. Even at that sad moment Ralph needed to get off the phone with Isaac and keep fine-tuning with his new synthesizer.

~

Ann had long expected when the time came, she would take over the role of Sadie in the family. She would advise her father and steady him in his old age. In a sense, she had been training for this the many unpleasant years living with Sherman. It was the natural order of things. She believed Isaac was a resourceful and energetic businessman—believed this almost as a religious truth. Her father had risen from poverty with no education and had made a fortune for their family, a kind of miracle, and Ann tried not to think about distasteful details. Perhaps now with peace returning to the house Isaac could think properly again. Maybe something could still be salvaged. In this light, Ann could accept the puzzling death of her mother. She would help her father. She dreamed, maybe there could still be a happy ending.

For Shelley Silverman, the passing of Sadie fully opened the trapdoor to all her passions. She told Isaac she needed to build a luxury apartment on top of their garage in Rye, and she wanted to take her kids out of public school and enroll the five of them in costly Rye Country Day. Each day she had another bold and wonderful idea. By the pool in the romantic light of sunset, she mentioned she'd like to have a new white BMW convertible. He could trade in her year-old four-door sedan or keep it as a spare car, whatever he thought was best. Isaac stood beside her at sunset, nodding, thoughtfully considering.

Isaac was borrowing from everyone he knew to keep his young wife looking and feeling rich. He couldn't say no to her and still be the man she wanted. Shelley was his life, his youth. Meanwhile, the bank had foreclosed on Isaac's massive White Plains property and would soon sell it at auction. That factory had been the garden of his dreams. Just months before, he had been the owner of the IBM building. But Isaac couldn't say no to Shelley. Of course, she knew just the right moment after coffee and dessert to mention that in the future she wanted to be called "mother" by Ralph and Ann.

"Mother!" Ralph giggled a little when his father told him.

"Mother!" This modest request drove Ann to the edge of madness. She couldn't summon any words to answer her father and felt bile coming into her mouth. They were virtually the same age. Ann knew right then everything was lost. With her father living nearly full-time now with his other family, Ann, Sherman, and the kids were alone in the Riverdale house. This was poison for her. Ann would not be replacing her mother. Isaac's new wife had a different kind of power—power without wisdom or restraint. She only wanted more and more expensive things. Ann's father, her hero, had become a lunatic servant. He'd become a vehicle to enable this new wife's meretricious dreams. It was all gone. There were still three old buildings left in lower Manhattan, but they were ghost ships.

But also, this preposterous request of Isaac's trophy wife brought Ann to her senses. It changed the course of her life.

~

One morning, before dawn, drifting off to sleep Ralph had a vision of the parakeet that had once been his closest friend. He watched it resting on his shoulder, chatting with him before he left for school. When Ralph came home, his little friend was gone. He looked all over the house for the bird but couldn't find it. His mother told him the little bird had flown out the window, but Ralph didn't believe her. In Ralph's vision, he found his friend in the garbage. Ralph had this thought: His mother had disappeared from her house just like his parakeet.

Days later, when Ralph asked his sister about this premonition, she said to him, "Many things have disappeared from our house. . . . Sherman and Dad have ways of making things disappear." Ann wouldn't say anything more.

"Sadie was in his way," Ralph said to me decades later. "My father knew many people who would take care of this for him," He just needed to make a phone call.

To this day, Ralph believes his father had his mother murdered.

~

Nine months later before beginning her new life, Ann needed to save her baby brother, and she was pressed for time. When she arrived at Ralph's apartment on York Avenue, Ralph opened the door, and then as if he hadn't noticed his sister standing in the hall, he quickly returned to his desk in a corner of the living room and continued studying math equations on the screen or perhaps it was logic, she couldn't tell what he was doing. The place smelled of garbage, filthy dishes, and rank clothes and bedding. Every dish in the place was unwashed in the sink and on the kitchen table, and dirty dishes and silverware had spread into the living room where Ralph continued to work as if she weren't there.

Ann tried to steady herself reading the names of strange-looking objects, several Proto boards with a jumble of circuitry, two tape recorders, an ARP synthesizer, his new computer, something called a function generator, several tape decks, cassettes for data storage, hi-fi speakers that seemed to be linked together, and other things that had purposes she couldn't imagine. She tried to calm her racing mind. Ann was about to begin a new life, but first she needed to help her brother. She had always looked out for Ralph.

Ann and Ralph had four hours before their flight to Miami, and she needed to get her brother packed and out of his apartment and into a cab for JFK, but she couldn't get him to budge. From the computer, he briefly turned to his sister and said his work was crucial and he implored her not to disturb him.

Ralph hadn't paid his apartment rent in five months. He had no money for rent, hardly any money at all. Ann noticed an envelope resting on a small antique end table partially obscured by a coffee cup. She opened the envelope and took a quick look at the eviction notice. Isaac's business had now been foreclosed and liquidated. He'd been locked out of his downtown Manhattan office for weeks. Also, the bank had foreclosed on the Riverdale house, and Sherman, Ann, and their four kids were now living in a cramped two-family house in the Bronx, similar to the one where Ralph and Ann had grown up.

She tried to maintain a relaxed and even tone of voice. "You need to pack a few clothes, Ralph. We have less than two hours to leave here." He shook his head no. He was concentrating.

"You need to pack a few things, Ralph. Where we're going, there isn't much room." It was impossible to gain his attention. Ann had never been in this apartment before when her brother was working. He was in another world, but she was also in another world. In three days, Ann would be leaving the States for good. She had been planning her escape for months, perhaps subliminally for years. Sherman and her four children didn't know she was leaving and likely would never see her again. They didn't have a clue. While her baby brother fiddled with his equations or whatever they were, she allowed herself the fantasy of escaping Sherman's appalling embrace and life talk of skimming and payoffs. For months, Ann had been squirreling away money. She felt alive in a way she couldn't remember and didn't think was still possible. But first she needed to take her brother away from here and feel good about where he was settled. Jean had guided Ralph around for a half dozen years, but now she was gone. Sadie was gone. Isaac was too preoccupied to care about Ralph if he ever had. They didn't have much time.

"Ralph, look at me. Look at me. Please." Finally, he turned around. She was holding the eviction notice in her hand. "You haven't paid the rent here in five months. Tomorrow or perhaps on Wednesday, the police will bang on your door. If you don't answer, they will break the door down and come into your apartment. They will go through each of your rooms gathering up your belongings, your equipment, cassettes, all this stuff, and heave it onto the street. You will have nothing left. What you can't carry in your arms will go into the garbage. They will put a lock on your door. Do you understand? We have to leave here soon before the police come. You can take an hour and put a few things together for our trip. Gather some clothes. I'll bring you to a nice place where you can work." At this Ralph seemed to emerge from his equations or whatever they were. He gestured around the room at his treasures. To leave this place, he needed his computer and many cassettes, his protoboards, speakers, and all the rest. This was his work. He couldn't leave it. Ralph had been reconfiguring his computer, increasing its calculating speed so that he could better do advanced work in logic. He needed his speakers. He needed all these things. Don't you understand?

No, in her mind Ann had already traveled across the Atlantic to a new life. She still had many things to decide. It was almost unbearable for her to slow down and reason with him.

But finally, she agreed he could take his computer and some cassettes along with his clothes. And that was it. There was no room where he was going for more than some clothes and the computer.

No one in the world but Ann could have pried him out of that apartment. He trusted her. They would make a new life together. Ann had always watched out for Ralph, and he assumed she always would. He had no idea at all what she was planning. No one did.

Part III

My sister didn't talk much on the flight to Miami. She was pre-occupied, and so was I. Ann had always been in my corner and I trusted her. She was taking me to Florida to live with a distant cousin, but I wasn't thinking much about this. She could have taken me to the North Pole. I had my computer and a few note-books. Ann said I would have a quiet room to do my work.

The recent work with my new computer was opening my eyes to possibilities in philosophy I could never have imagined. The work was pulling me ahead, but I wasn't sure exactly where I was traveling. More and more, modern philosophy was becoming like advanced mathematics, particularly work in analytic logic. Even the most respected academic philosophers with big reputations from studies in Plato, Descartes, or Santayana drew a blank look-ing at work of analytic philosophers that often resembled dense math equations. My friend Saul Kripke, a true math genius, was at the forefront of this extremely esoteric field. But at that time, Kripke knew little about computers, and neither did Bob Weingard. I needed to do more work and then share ideas with my friends. I was certain computers would lead the way to breakthrough ideas in philosophy. That's where I was focused when my sister and I climbed out of a taxi with my computer and two suitcases and rang the doorbell of a small 1950s Spanish-style house located in Bay Harbor Islands.

Branden, in his early twenties, wearing Bermudas, flip-flops and a T-shirt, opened the front door with a snarky grin that brought me back into the moment. My sister was smiling and gracious, as always helping me put my best foot forward. A few hellos and then Branden guided us through his living room pausing to look out the large picture window, appreciating the view as if for the first time. He waited until Ann and I focused on his tricked-out Donzi speedboat hanging on davits above the Intracoastal behind the house. "That's my boat," he said, smiling broadly. "It looks fast," I said to be affable. "You bet it is. Real fast." I tried to smile enthusiastically. So did my sister.

He then led us to a small room off the living room. It was barely large enough for a single bed and a little end table. There was no closet or chest of drawers. Ann and I looked around trying to figure where to shove my suitcases. Branden knew that our father owned office buildings in Manhattan, but my sister hadn't mentioned Isaac's business had gone broke. She told me it might be better if I didn't tell our sad story to my Florida host. My cousin was a large presence in that little room. With a disdainful expression, he glanced at my notebooks spread across the narrow bed and my computer, most likely he'd never seen one before.

The room was dark, hardly more than a converted closet, with only one tiny window that looked as though it had been cut into the wall as an afterthought. But if Branden had sealed it off, I wouldn't have cared. I looked around wondering where I could set up my computer. I couldn't wait to get started.

Ann helped me place the computer on the end table and I was relieved that it fit. I needed a chair and maybe a second chair to pile my notebooks, then I could go to work. With my ideas beginning to percolate, my sister's impatience only barely registered. Then there was a moment of awkwardness—we were being pulled hard in different directions and neither Ann nor I could find any words. Then my sister gave me a hug and kiss and said she'd see me soon. I didn't think to ask her when or where she was going. I think Ann was a little teary, but I don't know, maybe that's just my memory playing tricks.

That was the last time I ever saw my sister Ann.

~

I'm sure my cousin Branden had high hopes for me because of my father's office buildings. Whenever I ran into him in the hall, we'd exchange a smile and I'd give him a thumbs-up to convey, yeah, everything in your house is really wonderful. He'd graduated from college two years earlier and talked about maybe going to law school but not with much conviction or enthusiasm. Clearly, he was looking for a way to edge himself into those buildings. I was Isaac's son, after all, a minor star or at least a gateway player. In fairness to my cousin, why else would he have told my sister I could come here and live in his house? What was in it for him? This had never been explained to me.

That first night, when I ran into him in the kitchen, Branden asked, "So how is Isaac doing?" as if they'd once been buddies.

"He's doing terrific," I answered, and then grabbed an apple from the refrigerator and headed back to my room. I felt badly about that. I knew I should have had something more to say.

But really, I had no idea how my father was doing. All of that had fallen behind a dark curtain—the young wife, the five kids, the pool built by Sammy Gravano. I had no idea what was going on there.

I mostly stayed in my room. I was focused on a logical paradox I'd often discussed with Weingard called the sorites paradox, but I wasn't making much headway. I was feeling frustrated. I knew that to be welcome in this house I'd need to be prepared to say something more about the buildings. Truth was that Dad's old buildings had never seemed very important or attractive to me. In the end, they'd brought much pain to my family, and I tried best as I could to put them out of my mind.

From the living room, there was usually the sound of football on the tube and a lot of cheering and cursing from Branden's college buddies. That was okay, because I had headphones and I was absorbed in my work.

Most afternoons and late into the night, the smell of marijuana was in the air, and if I happened to open my door and glance into the living room, the air was foggy with it. For almost two years now, since I'd started working on Pythagoron, marijuana had become toxic to me. It impeded my thinking, and I could no longer tolerate the smell. I stuffed towels under the door of my tiny room to block the smoke, put on my headphones, and tried to work.

Branden and I were living separate lives. That was okay with me. Around midnight, when the living room quieted down, I made my way into the kitchen and looked for fruit in the refrigerator. I hadn't tasted meat for three years. I could usually find a few oranges, grapes, or an apple in the fridge. There was a sweet little black-and-white cat living in the house. On nights when I came to the kitchen for fruit, the cat seemed to be waiting there for me, rubbed against my legs, and then followed me back to my room when I returned with the fruit. I called him Gato and we became friends.

Then one day, there was knocking on my door when I was deep into the seemingly impenetrable sorites paradox and could not bear to wrest myself away. My cousin pushed open the door, which jolted me, and then he kicked aside the three or four towels I had stuffed in the crack at the bottom of the door to keep the smell out. He gave me a surprised look about the towels. I told him that the smell of grass made it hard for me to do my work. I was trying to be congenial, but maybe that wasn't the best thing to say.

Then Branden really surprised me. He was holding a large paper bag with grease dripping from the bottom. He looked at my unmade bed, shook his head trying to figure out the best thing to do. I couldn't imagine what he had in mind. Finally he reached down to the floor and tossed the towels onto the bed. Then he opened the bag and took out two greasy boxes, one filled with egg rolls and the other with spareribs.

Branden had brought a gift. He spilled the ribs and egg rolls onto the towels and invited me to dig in. But the stuff was disgusting to me. For years I had been a vegetarian. The smell of his greasy food nauseated me. I didn't know what to do. It would be like eating dog shit. Branden was looking at me, waiting for me to dig in. I needed to tell him I couldn't eat this stuff, but I felt tension growing in him. He was chewing on a rib, waiting for me to get started.

If he could accept my passions and habits, why couldn't I accept his? This was in the air along with the smell of cheap Chinese takeout. I had no choice. I grabbed a sparerib and began eating, telling myself, that years before I had loved these things. I had to eat it. I was eating for my life.

As I took a second bite of a sparerib, I tried to look happy. Branden looked over at my computer wondering what the hell was going on in his house. There was a scattering of symbols on the screen. Maybe he thought I was a terrorist. I knew I had to say something about what he was looking at on the computer. Some explanation. Something. "It's a way of processing abstract symbolic information" I said with grease dripping from my lips. "That's what computers do."

Maybe I'd need to eat this stuff and smoke dope to survive here. What else could I do? I was living in his house. I was doing philosophy and had a roof over my head. And maybe this was just a rough patch and in time Branden could grow to respect my work and leave me alone. Computers would soon change the way all of us live in the world. I knew this as clearly as I knew my hand, but Branden could have cared less. I stuffed an egg roll into my mouth and nodded, "Good, real good."

Branden smiled at me as if we were making progress. "We'll go out for a spin in the boat," he said, leaving my tiny room as I smiled and nodded yes.

Living in the Harbor Islands house with Branden and his buddies was like living on the end of a tree branch, but I still didn't get it. Not yet. I was doing work I valued and had a roof over my head. I still hoped maybe in time Branden could come to respect my work.

Interesting when you think about it. The work I was doing in Branden's place was at its core about language, the precise meaning of language. And it was language that ultimately broke us.

I didn't see much of Branden for the next few days or maybe a week or more. Time was flying by. I was finally doing good work on the computer. At midnight, when the coast was clear, I walked quietly to the kitchen, talked to the cat, and foraged for fruit. A couple of times, I made late-night whispering phone calls to Weingard, and we shared ideas about the sorites paradox. Bob never asked me where I was living or with whom, but I didn't expect he would. He only wanted to hear about my ideas, and I wanted to hear his. While Gato rubbed against my legs, I spoke to Weingard about how useful the computer was for doing linguistic analysis and urged him to buy a machine, but he was noncommittal about this. Weingard and I were both renegades. We did work in our own way and weren't easily persuaded. Maybe that's part of what made us so close.

Then one night, Branden again pushed my door open holding another bag of Chinese takeout. Same routine. "You're gonna fuckin' love this," he said, dumping the food and grease on some towels he tossed on my bed. "This is fuckin' great. Try the duck." He handed me a piece of duck that looked half raw, but what the hell, I put it in my mouth.

"Fuckin' great, no?"

I was trying to eat a little without vomiting. I couldn't understand how he ate this stuff night after night. This was the price of survival.

"Fuckin' delicious, yeah?"

That's when I noticed that in every third or fourth sentence Branden said, "Fuckin'." "Fuckin' beautiful night." "Fuckin' great game." "Fuckin' piece of ass." "Fuckin' great tits." "Fuckin' great duck?"

This disgusted me even more than the duck. I couldn't bear the way Branden spoke. His use of language made me feel crazy. I must have said something that upset him. I can't really remember. My computer felt like a lifeline I needed to grab to save myself. I was about to turn back to my computer when Branden slapped me in the face. Hard. That was the first time he hit me.

"You're a fuckin' asshole," he said, leaving my room and slamming the door.

"Fuckin' asshole." It kept drumming in my head. I couldn't even look at the fuckin' computer the rest of the night.

I tried to analyze what had gone wrong. My cousin thought he could use me as an asset. He knew my dad owned office buildings in Manhattan. He couldn't bear it that I wouldn't open the door to those buildings so he could walk into the office and sit at a big, polished mahogany desk signing up tenants and banking his fortune. He thought that was my part of our deal, like paying rent.

I just needed to open that fuckin' door for him to stroll through. "Why? Fuckin' why, Ralph?"

I had been pondering the sorites paradox without caring about Branden, his needs, his values, his friends, his sex life. I never once visited his friends in the living room. Not once. I wouldn't smoke grass with them. I couldn't talk about pro football and business schemes. I couldn't even fake it. I should have felt Branden's frustration, sitting in the living room watching the games with his buddies when his big dreams were only a soft toss away down the hall to my door.

I must have been a terrible frustration to Branden. Those fuckin' buildings were the very meaning of life. "You're such a fuckin' asshole, Ralph. Why won't you fuckin' help me?" That's why he slapped me.

Sometimes, Branden was decent and friendly for a few hours or for a day or two, but then turned on a dime and became violent. Once I mentioned to him that a steady diet of greasy food might not be the best thing, and he screamed at me, "What the fuck is wrong with you, Ralph? Can't you fuckin' hear me?" I didn't hear him, couldn't hear him. Not really. I was into a different realm that he could never understand. How could I ever explain myself to Branden? I couldn't explain me to myself. Maybe I smiled or something and he shoved me onto the bed.

Sherman. That's what came to me one night when I was trying to focus on the sorites paradox. Branden wanted to be Sherman. He wanted to skim and scheme and chisel and work the contractors for kickbacks. I was living with Sherman. My sister had left me marooned with Sherman. I tried to smile and be pleasant. Branden thought I was ignoring his ideas about fuckin' cool women and cool dressing. He didn't like my lack of concern about grooming. And I guess, in fairness, I smelled and so did the sheets and underwear in my room. He screamed at me that I was fuckin' bringing him down. I tried to be positive and pleasant. I was so excited about my ideas.

But I just drove him crazy.

One day, he started slapping me in the face for no good reason. My glasses fell to the floor, and one of the lenses shattered and the other broke in the middle. As I reached for my glasses, he continued slapping me. Then he screamed my name as if I was living on another planet and he was trying to bridge the distance. Maybe he was right about this. Maybe he was seeing what I couldn't see.

But mainly Branden saw me as an impediment, I wouldn't let him into those fuckin' buildings. I was someone who didn't pay off. Someone who wasn't paying his way. Or worse, someone who made him feel stupid.

Part IV

In the early evening, Branden came into my room and pulled me out of my chair. I had been working an idea and getting close. I wanted to call Weingard to see what he thought. Branden pulled me through the living room where a few of his friends were drinking beer. He opened the front door and pushed me out onto the lawn. I wasn't wearing my shoes. I only had some change in a pocket along with my broken glasses.

I began walking aimlessly. Branden's house was on a lovely block with palm and mango trees and beautiful homes I'd never noticed before. I wanted to stay here and rest, but I sensed I couldn't. I didn't know where to go or which way I was headed. I didn't know the neighborhood at all. I'd been living my life in my room analyzing language. That's where I was comfortable. My work was there. My mind drifted to an idea I had been working on with Weingard. I felt there was a solution near at hand. I felt like calling him to discuss it. But how could I call him? No phone. No money. This was preposterous, I knew that much. I had no shoes. I thought about going back for my shoes but confronting Branden again seemed too perilous. My glasses were broken. I could barely see without my glasses. My girlfriend had moved back to New Hampshire. I didn't have her new phone number. She hadn't given it to me. I didn't understand why. My sister had left home for somewhere. When I last tried to call my father, I was told he wasn't living in the house in Rye anymore. I had no idea where he was staying. I had no idea where I was going.

But the air was cool and fresh, and without a hint of marijuana.

~

Several blocks from Branden's house I came across a tiny park near the water, just a few benches on a patch of lawn facing the canal, an inviting place with lights from houses glimmering on the waterway. Such a shame I'd never noticed this place before. It would have been lovely to escape the blasting television and smell of marijuana at Branden's, a place to relax and think. I put my feet up and began to close my eyes. I must have dozed off when someone kicked my feet hard with a shoe. What the . . . I woke up confused with two policemen looming over me. One of them said, "Pull your stuff together an get outta here."

What stuff? I had no stuff. I had nothing.

"If I see you here again, I'm going to take you in."

"Yes, sir, I'm sorry. I'm just leaving, Officer."

But I wanted to ask these guys where should I go? That's something you can ask the police, but I didn't dare.

While they watched me, I tried to walk away decisively like a homeowner on Bay Harbor. But I'd been living for weeks in a tiny room in front of my computer and had lost all sense of direction, I'd even forgotten I was staying on an island. After walking a little further along the water, I could make out a small bridge ahead.

When I arrived at the bridge, I paused to take stock. Should I go right or left? To my left, there were two clumps of fuzzy lights, one larger and brighter. I was trying to get my bearings. But I kept thinking about my feet and the sweet little friend Gato I'd left behind. Going into Miami felt like the wrong choice. How could I make my way in the city without shoes? I moved off toward the clump of softer lights.

But I wasn't really sure what I was looking at. Strong lights. Softer lights. I walked barefoot and confused across the bridge. Probably further away was Miami. Everything was cloudy and distorted except for a sliver on the right side of the right lens of my glasses. I'd need to calm myself so I could think properly. Weingard and I were planning to coauthor a paper on the sorites paradox. But I couldn't recall my conclusion.

I headed where the lights seemed softer, less threatening, must be Miami Beach. It was only a glow but somehow it felt familiar. I'd gone on vacation there four or five times with Isaac, Sadie, and Ann.

I kept walking and after a while I came onto Collins Avenue, put my right eye almost onto on the street sign to be sure. Yes, Collins Avenue.

I walked along Collins trying to identify places I'd visited with my parents and Ann years before. Mother occasionally allowed us to eat at Wolfie's because Isaac loved the chopped chicken liver sandwiches, though she much preferred the Rascal House, open twenty-four hours and offering free rolls and pickles. The Rascal House was favored by clientele who enjoyed the Catskills in the summers, and Mom felt more at home there. This was a Jewish area. I could somehow fit in here.

I was headed south where the better hotels are located. I was drawn to upscale places. It was the only life I'd ever known before my unhappy weeks with Branden. I started walking with a more confident gait. Fred had stayed at the Fontainebleau, with his father, and told me about beautiful women arriving in fancy convertibles all day and night. I would have loved to have seen that, but Sadie would never allow our family to go to the Fontainebleau. Only reform Jews stayed there. Spending even one night there would bring years of bad luck to our family. Sadie liked the Seagull Hotel. I was heading for the Seagull right on the beach. I felt such nostalgia recalling my mom holding up her skirt to waddle into the ocean at the Seagull.

It seemed like I'd been walking for hours. For some reason, I hadn't come to Wolfie's or the Sea Gull Hotel. Maybe they were on the other side of the street, and I walked right past them. I asked a lady where the Seagull Hotel was located, but she looked me over and didn't answer. I kept walking. My feet were killing me.

I soon came to a public park with many trees, benches, and stretches of lawn where I could make out men and women laying on blankets. I was too tired to make it to the Seagull. This looked like a good place to pause. I thought about resting on a park bench, but recalling my recent episode, I instead leaned against a tree and stretched out. My feet were hurting and chilled despite the warm evening.

I'd lucked out in a way. There were regular people here, sitting on the lawn, chatting on benches, couples enjoying the evening breeze off the Intracoastal. No drunks or vagrants asking for handouts that I could see. Nobody seemed to notice me.

I needed to eat and go to the bathroom but to keep myself from obsessing about food I began thinking about binary numbers and doing exercises in my head. I needed to learn much more about binary number theory to do the advanced computer study that was crucial to my work.

I was exhausted and half asleep when a man began speaking to me. I could barely make out his features in the darkness.

"Been out here long? What are you doing here?"

"I was thrown out of the house I was living in," I answered like someone else was talking—words just flew out of me. "I didn't know what to do."

"Here's couple of dollars," he said, putting two singles in my hand.

I thought about saying no, but I was already holding the dollars, so I figured, why not. It was like playing a game. I'd soon track down my dad's new phone number and this difficulty would be resolved.

I walked behind a bunch of nearby bushes and took a crap. Then I went back to leaning against the tree and closed my eyes.

In the morning when I woke up, laying near my feet, there was a pair of worn pale blue dress loafers with a tassel. They fit, sort of.

I splashed water on my face from a nearby fountain and set off in my new shoes walking south for about a mile until I came to a phone booth within hailing distance of the Fontainebleau hotel. I'd intended to place a call to my father, but during the walk along the Intracoastal, my head cleared and the work I'd been doing for months on the sorites paradox suddenly came sharply into focus. I was amazed how clearly I understood it right then beside the waterway. I needed to tell Weingard and also Saul Kripke if I could reach him at Princeton. The argument I'd arrived at was very dense, but in the end I discovered the sorites paradox was a problem without a solution. That was the solution. It was unsolvable. Weingard and I had worked on this for months searching for a solution when there was none to find. Amazing how a night's sleep and a refreshing walk along the water can change one's mood and ability to think.

I was so excited to share my analysis with Weingard, but after he accepted my collect call, he just wasn't terribly interested, and instead of hearing me out he began talking about a problem in physics he'd been mulling over. I hemmed and hawed trying to maneuver Weingard back to the sorites solution, but I already knew the moment was lost. Weingard always goes his own way. If I'd mentioned my difficulty with Branden and my present dilemma, he would have become impatient because such digressions interfered with the real stuff of life. Finally, he said to me, "Ralph, I can't work on sorites anymore. You can do anything you want with it. Use any of the ideas we discussed. Feel free to write the paper yourself." Then for the next ten or fifteen minutes, he lost me in an issue of physics that, frankly, I didn't care about. In the end, I could feel that I had disappointed him. When I got off with Weingard, I wandered back toward the park in a dejected state.

On the way I stopped at a deli and spent my two dollars on a small container of cottage cheese and a tiny box of raisins that I ate with my fingers while walking north along the water. I hadn't eaten much of anything for two days, and before I reached the park I was still famished. I couldn't find the damn tree where I'd slept the night before, which made me nervous, so I sat on a bench. I was hungry and bummed out from my call to Weingard. I'd thought of us as a team making important discoveries in philosophy. Doing this work without Weingard felt so goddamned lonely. I fought against these sad ideas by doing practice exercises with binary numbers.

Eventually I became bored and decided to look around the surrounding area. Near the canal, not far from where I was sitting, vagrants sprawled on the grass, some of them muttering to one another and sipping from cans, beer probably. A few were smoking and from the smell, it was weed. Several moved around slowly as if they were punch drunk. Regular people seemed to stay clear of this area of the park.

Of course, with my broken glasses, there was much speculation about my surroundings and neighbors. I was guessing, sensing, or trying to, like a cat. People must have thought I was unbalanced strolling around the park sticking the right side of my glasses up close to people's faces or to trees to catch a glimpse of where I was and who was there.

I had the impression that some people living in this sorrowful place had been recently prosperous and didn't know what had happened to them. They seemed confused or absent as if they had been dumped here like garbage bags. Or they'd been bombed out of their homes and had to suddenly deal with being homeless and didn't know how. I imagined it was a terrible shock like the first day in the army. Folks trying to superimpose an understanding they once had from another life. I didn't know what the rules were in this strange land, what was appropriate. What do I say to people I meet in the park? Do I greet them or remain silent like a shadow?

In the larger area of the park, there were couples holding hands and ladies pushing strollers with smiling babies waving at passersby. Jean had never wanted to have a baby. She had always known the right thing to do. But we were still young. Maybe she could still change her mind. I waved back at one little girl and her mother quickly pushed her away from me. I couldn't find my damn tree so I settled for another. I must not have looked very good. A lady gave me a dollar and I said thank you. I didn't know where I fit in. What the hell had I been doing looking for the Seagull Hotel? What would I have done there if I'd found it?

~

Hours slipped past like minutes. I'm not sure how long I was leaning against the tree, six hours, two days? Time, weather, boredom,
hunger merged to a single entity. I had seemed to have lost the
motivation to work on philosophy. Whenever I collected two dollars, I walked to the deli for cottage cheese and raisins, but it was
never enough, and hunger settled into my being like breathing. I
missed the little cat I'd befriended at Branden's. My hours would
have been so much more pleasant if I'd carried Gato off with me,
but that was also in the past. My home had become a tree not
far from the area the where the homeless lived. There were some
nearby bushes where I relieved myself. I never asked anyone for
a handout, but I always nodded yes and muttered thanks when it
was offered.

Soon enough, I'd walk back to the Fontainebleau and call my
dad on the phone. He'd send money and I'd be back in New York,
studying and writing philosophy, living as I had for most of my
life. But meanwhile, I decided I should dip into this world in the
park, learn what it's about. I felt a surge of excitement at this idea
of being an observer or voyeur. Living like a bum was an opportunity few people like me would ever have in a lifetime like climbing Mount Everest.

A few days after my call to Weingard, a towering black man
came over to the tree and looked me over. He seemed to be staring at my T-shirt. Maybe because it had become filthy during days
living on the ground. This guy's arms were thick as a big man's

thighs. I smiled at him to be friendly. He was looking me over like a hero sandwich.

"You're a Crip," he said finally.

"Huh?"

"If anyone asks you, you say you're a Crip, understand?"

I was confused by this.

'You're my kind of people," he said.

"How can you tell?"

"I could tell by your blue T-shirt. You and I are both Crips."

I nodded. My kind of people. This was incredible.

"Blue is okay. White is okay. But never wear red."

"Okay, I answered. "I'll never wear red."

"If you wear red, you could find yourself in a blood bath."

I was wearing the only shirt I had with me so this shouldn't be a worry.

He went on, "No one gets through this life alone. You'll need protection. Understand?"

I didn't understand, but I nodded yes.

"You must never wear red. Always the blue shirt," he repeated. "If anyone asks you, you tell 'em, you're a Crip."

"I'm happy you told me this," I said while he was digesting my hand in his hand as large as a baseball mitt.

We shook and nodded in agreement. I was a Crip. Then he stumbled off in the direction of the canal.

Leaning against my tree, I couldn't get over this chance meeting that was so off the wall but also had me thinking. I had no idea about the rules of survival here. I recalled an afternoon several years earlier sitting in a cozy wood-paneled library in Pennsylvania with Jean who was doing research for her Ph.D. She was quietly translating aloud from a copy of an ancient Greek text called *The Secret History* that focused on the reign of Justinian and Theodora as emperor and empress of the Byzantine Empire. Jean had often said that ancient civilizations weren't so different from our own and there were many lessons to learn from them. Jean was so much more comfortable and confident in the worlds of animals and ancients. I found this charming and wacky and I loved her for it. Anyway, as she'd read from the historian Procopius, I'd been astounded by the splendor and violence of the Byzantine Empire. I recalled in particular one section of the history about gangs that ruled the streets. Gang members were identified by colors, usually blues and greens. There were gruesome slaughters that had taken place between gangs, thousands were killed, and getting up in the morning and forgetting to put on the right color tunic had often meant the difference between life and death.

"To survive here you've got to be something," the huge man had said to me before wandering off into the homeless section of the park. "You've got to be something to survive here," he repeated.

~

Perhaps the big man's warning affected me more than I realized because now I hardly strayed from my tree. I mostly stopped eating because it felt like such a chore to walk to the deli for cottage cheese and raisins that hardly made a difference in my hunger. A few homeless neighbors must have noticed. From time to time a resident of the park would hand me a piece of fruit or a buttered roll. But if I didn't eat at all, it hardly seemed to matter. I was used to starving. In my first homeless days I thought about eating as something optional. I felt detached from the distress of the situation I was in. I was like a child trying to understand the world he was discovering, the world almost literally at arm's length.

But I didn't think it was fear that kept me moored in place. Rather, I'd fallen into a kind of trance or fascination with the aesthetics of my world beside the tree.

Looking closely at my surroundings had become my work. I found a half tube of artist's red oil paint in the garbage. I put my eye close to the lip of the tube and slowly squeezed. I watched the thick oil paint curling into a sculpture on the dirt. Another day I found a rusty gasoline automobile pump that had been tossed. I studied it, felt it with my hands, tried to imagine inventing it myself. The complexity of small things was a new world.

Through my broken glasses, the world seemed splintered like my recent life. But when I took my glasses off and put my eye close to a flower or a blade of grass or a clump of dirt, I made discoveries. I became fascinated by the details of ordinary things that we would usually ignore.

When I laid the right edge of my glasses against my skin or a twig, it acted like a magnifying glass. For hours I studied reeds and twigs and the ruts and crevices on my wrist through the remaining shard of my glasses. Breaking a cigarette in half and looking at it through my glass, it appeared like a contagion of coiled snakes. I saw things I'd never noticed before. These things loomed larger than life for me. I fell into the beauty of little things.

One day I was staring close to the ground when a girl stopped by on her bike and asked me what I was doing. I was flummoxed not having spoken to anyone for several days. I felt like an idiot trying to explain to her why I had my nose almost touching the dirt. I stammered a bit trying to explain that I was looking closely at grass and flowers. The girl's name was Sandy. She was coming from the beach where she sold sunglasses to make a few dollars, but she liked to spend time in the park.

She was very sweet. Like a big kitten. She reminded me of the cat I'd left behind at Branden's house. I said a little more about the grass and flowers. When she offered a joint to share, I felt too embarrassed to say no. Sandy was ethereal, dreamy, half in another world. I could go for her. But she had a boyfriend who lived in one of the fancy condominiums by the ocean. Too bad. She told me that she had been a graduate student at Columbia in fine arts before moving down here. Then she said, "Gotta go," and left as abruptly as she appeared, giving me a wave as she headed off on her bike toward the canal where the homeless lived. That seemed strange.

A few days later I was back staring at the ground when Sandy came by a second time on her bike.

"Ha, still looking at the dirt!" she announced. "What ya seeing there?"

"Seeing things I've never seen before."

For the second time, she told me she lived with her boyfriend in one of the high-rise condos on the beach but came to the park sometimes to hang out. Sandy was drawing a line, needed me to know she wasn't a homeless girl. But it was okay. When she came by to visit, the world brightened for me.

"Why'd you leave school?" I asked her.

"I just got bored with it, so I'm taking a break. But I'll go back when I feel like it. Finish my degree and teach some place like Vassar or Swarthmore."

"What have you been seeing today?" she asked.

"Looking up close at the head of a tiny paintbrush." I handed her the brush and she shrugged, so what.

"Yeah, but when you look at it through the glass, it looks like a woman's hair streaming in the wind. When the sun catches the glass at the right angle, it looks like her hair is on fire."

"Can I take a look?"

Sandy visited me two or three times. There were always unanswered questions. Why had she left school? Did she really have a boyfriend in one of the big condominiums? Why did she ride off to the homeless village when she left me?

Sandy told me that her parents owned a large estate in Connecticut, not far from Paul Newman's house. From her description, it dwarfed the Errol Flynn estate. Sandy needed me to know she was in a different league. This was basic to our nascent friendship.

She and I looked at many things under the broken glass: butterfly wings, grass, the head of a match, clumps of dirt, ants looking like monsters with giant eyes. Then one day she said to me, "Let me look at your eye."

I turned so she could see my eye. "Not like that silly."

Sandy put my glasses on and leaned in toward my face. "I can't see, need to come closer," she said. So she did. She was so close that her nose was touching mine and her eye twisted to the side was practically touching my eye.

"That's so cool," she said, speaking right into my mouth.

"What do you see?"

"From a couple inches away, it's just an eye, nothing special. But when the piece of glass is almost touching your eyeball, it looks like a kaleidoscope, but more beautiful, much more intimate." She kept moving her eye against mine. "Sometimes it's dark and scary, and sometimes just beautiful webbing of colors depending on the angle in the sun. Want to try?"

So I put on my glasses and bent into her eye, again nuzzling noses though I tried not to. Her eye kept changing with the angle of our faces. In one moment, it looked like it was on fire. After a small adjustment, it looked like a piece of knitting art and then like an open vagina. She giggled when I told her this. We kept trading off, looking deeply into one another's eyes. It must have looked sexual, and in truth, it was very arousing.

We were both into it, eye to eye with our noses caressing, breathing into each other as we turned our heads in a kind of dance to catch the sun from a different angle. But I guess she sensed I was getting hot, knew just the moment to push me away.

"See you," she said, getting back on her bike to visit friends in the homeless village before returning to her boyfriend in the condo by the sea.

~

One night I heard the sound of music coming from the canal. I got up and moved away from my tree as if I'd never been stuck there. I wandered in among the homeless who were dancing to Marvin Gaye from a cheap boom box. Through my broken glasses they looked like shadow dancers. I sat on the lawn and felt the sway of the music. Someone passed me half a ham sandwich and I ate it voraciously. The weather was warm and balmy with palms moving in the breeze. I felt like I'd been released from a cage. Someone passed me a joint and I drew in deeply. After a minute or two I felt the rush. It was so good I wanted more. At Branden's, the smell had disgusted me. It must have been the breeze off the water. Or Marvin Gaye. I watched the dancers. I had never been good at dancing but watching had always been a delight. Then I noticed a couple nearby fucking on the lawn. The girl beside me kept passing the joint while the music swept up into the swaying palms. Smoking weed in the park was wonderful. It felt like a new life. The girl kept passing the joint. Why not, I nodded happily. I noticed girls occasionally leading men by the hand in the direction of the woman's bathroom. I would have loved to have taken my turn, but who should I ask about this? The girl handed me the joint and when I offered it back, she signaled, no you keep it. Marvin Gaye never sounded so good as through that cheap boom box. My neighbor lay down beside me on the grass, seemed to give me an impish smile but I couldn't see her clearly. I imagined she was cuter than hell. She must have been. I was feeling the soft wind on my face when she slowly pulled down my zipper and reached in with her hand. Oh my, but is this allowed here? I flashed briefly on the huge black man, you can find yourself in a blood bath, but by then she had taken me into her mouth. I hadn't had sex in months. A soft delicious moment in the evening breeze with the sadness of Marvin Gaye all through that sad park. I'd always thought he was pleading to his violent father and to my father.

Must have been her boyfriend standing over me with a clenched fist. I couldn't make out his face, but I felt the spit falling from his mouth onto my face. He was gonna kill me. Right here in homeless village, still that yearning music, I didn't want to let it go. I reached to pull up the zipper on my pants. But he grabbed my wrist like a vise. He could toss me into the canal with the bull sharks or rip my penis off. Who would ever know or care? Should have stayed by my tree looking at the grass. "I'm gonna kill you, mother fucker. Messing with my girl." She had taken off. Just me and her guy. This was it for me. Now the music had stopped, or at least I could no longer hear it. "That was my girl. What the fuck were you thinking?"

I wasn't thinking.

"I didn't know, man. I'm so sorry. What can I do? Just a mistake. Terrible mistake."

"Give me what you got?"

He wanted money. I had nothing. I told him. He was about to smash my face into the dirt.

"Wait, wait." I remembered a dollar bill an old lady had given to me a few days before. I pulled the crumpled dollar out of my pocket, put it in his hand, and then pulled my pockets inside out to show him, nothing else there.

I guess I was too pathetic to matter.

"Get outta here, mother fucker."

I nodded and took off for my tree.

~

Sandy was no longer around. I learned that the homeless in the park were a nomadic bunch. Residents would stay here for days or weeks, and then something called two or ten of them to disappear to other parks in Broward County, Palm Beach, or the northern Florida Keys, and some vagrants moved on to different parts of the country. Of course, I would never know about this firsthand. I was a sojourner in a foreign land, learning, watching, before returning to my scholarly life.

Sandy's occasional visits had primed me for pleasure but also opened the gates to boredom and anxiety. During long days sitting by my tree, binary math exercises no longer interested me. Years earlier I'd read about the Greek philosopher Eratosthenes who discovered that the earth was spherical by measuring shadows in different locations. He determined that the circumference of the earth was about 25,000 miles, which is remarkably accurate. I'd studied the formula that Eratosthenes used to make his calculations, but now I could no longer remember it. I was trying to re-create the idea while I was sitting under park trees, but I couldn't. This alarmed me. I began to worry about what else I was forgetting.

The weeks in the park were taking a toll. I was shedding weight and could barely keep my pants from falling to my knees. My stomach was burning, and instead of ideas I began thinking about food from the moment I woke up. Still I couldn't bring myself to beg for money. I lurched from my tree into the section of the park where the regular folks came to enjoy a sunny afternoon. I sat on a bench with my hands folded, looking down at my lap with a forlorn expression until someone put change or a dollar into my hand. Then I walked to the deli. Sometimes I needed to wait hours until I had enough for cottage cheese and raisins, and as the hurricane season was approaching, the sky often turned black while I waited for a handout. Then I raced to my tree before the sky opened up with lighting and torrential rain. Trees offered some cover, but I'd never experienced such rain before. In moments, I was soaked through and shivering. Then for hours, I was clammy and cold and then baking and sweating in my filthy rags, begging for a dollar or two, and before my clothing had dried, the rain came again. I was never completely dry, and yet my biggest worry, along with food, was water. I worried about the safety of taking a drink. All the homeless lapped from the same water fountain and often used it to clean themselves and I don't even want to think of what else. The little sink was filthy and smelled like a sewer. What kind of filth and germs was I taking in each time I took a sip?

~

One evening, I was sitting on a bench in the homeless section, half in a trance. It hadn't rained in two days and after the heat of the day, I was mostly dry but wretched from weeks without a shower. I couldn't stand the smell of my body. I promised myself to visit the beach and wash the following day. I'd been making this promise for a week. I didn't even notice when the huge black man, my friend from the Crips, settled beside me.

Then I heard two girls arguing, but I couldn't see them very well. One claimed the other had stolen her watch when they were in the bathroom. The larger one who now had the watch cursed the other out. They were going back and forth about the watch. Soon the two of them were rolling on the ground punching and clawing. I could only half imagine their battle in the darkness but the larger one was clearly getting the best of it. The smaller was soon exhausted and mainly holding on but the larger woman kept hitting her and cursing. Then the larger one dragged the other onto her feet, had the smaller by the neck and began slamming her head into the narrow top edge of a nearby park bench. I couldn't see much, but I could see this. The larger one was going to split the other's head open. Many homeless were watching, no one doing a thing. I didn't get it.

I stood up, took a step or two forward and the big guy beside me, my Crip buddy, grabbed my pants and pulled me back onto the bench. "Friend, in the park you can't touch a girl. Not even to stop a fight. If you grab a girl here, the police will fuck you up." He pushed me back onto the seat while the larger girl kept slamming the head of the other against the top rung of the bench. I recalled my sister being beaten and bleeding in the Bronx twenty-five years before while I just sat on the ground, watching, confounded, didn't know what to do. I still didn't know. Again I started to stand, and he pulled me back. "Want to spend months in jail?" Rules, so many rules. The beating went on for a long time, or so it seemed, but probably that was a loop I kept replaying in my head for days or months afterward. Maybe I could have pushed myself past the black guy and tried to stop it. I made a show of it but didn't try too hard, not really. I've often thought, how could I have just sat there? I might have saved her.

Finally the larger girl was finished with her fight. She turned her back on the scene and walked away without ever turning to take a look. The smaller one was half-sprawled on the bench with her feet dangling onto the grass. She was bleeding from the ears.

People stared for a minute or two, muttered a few words and then everyone moved away from these few moments and returned to their sorry places in the park. No one called the police or an ambulance. The park was soon silent and listless as if it never happened.

Enough. I'd seen enough. Much more than I wanted to see. I needed to leave this unforgiving place while I was still mostly okay.

~

The following morning, I trudged back to the phone booth with my legs feeling moored in concrete. The sight of the Fontainebleau in the distance held not even a smidgeon of allure. On this morning it seemed disgusting to me. There was nothing more for me in Miami Beach.

I was tired. I didn't even want to call Weingard. He wouldn't care about how I'd been living, not even about the girl. He'd want to talk about physics. I didn't want to feel annoyed with him.

My dad's wife picked up on the second ring. She wasn't pleased to take my collect call, but she did. Probably she'd been sitting by her poolside cabanas holding a mixed drink while sunning herself. Her voice was straining for self-importance. She curtly gave me Isaac's phone number and then hung up without another word as if I were a bum on the street. She'd always acted as if I was shit. But it amused me a little to think if she could see me now, smell me now.

I was so relieved when my dad picked up. "Ralphie," he nearly screamed my name as if his son had been lost at sea, and after all hope was gone I'd been found alive and well. That made me so fucking happy.

"Are you okay, Ralphie, I've been worried about you?"

"I'm okay, Dad. Fine I guess."

I asked him about Ann and he said, he hadn't heard from her for a while, she was off somewhere. I asked him where she was, I needed to speak to her, and then his voice trailed off as it had so many times in the past when I tried to talk to him about something and his focus suddenly turned to a problem he was having in one of the old buildings, a lease renewal or a broken motor in an elevator shaft.

"This life isn't for me, Dad."

I didn't know where to start. I needed to tell him about the weeks with Branden, that I'd lost my computer and all my notes. How could I get them back? I wanted to tell him about the girl in the park who was murdered and no one even cared. And Dad, you wouldn't believe how I look now. I need you to get me out of here. Dad, I need to come home. But I never had a chance to say any of it.

"Don't worry, Ralphie," my father said, quickly tying our lives in a ribbon.

"Soon we'll have plenty of money. There is nothing to worry about. Nothing at all."

My dad's new wife had thrown him out of the Errol Flynn estate, and he was now living in a tiny Section 8 apartment in Rye, New York. He had defrauded banks for hundreds of thousands to make mortgage payments on his old buildings. Now he was suing the government for twenty million dollars but more likely he was dreaming about suing the government for twenty million.

"Meanwhile you need to get along, Ralph."

Then an awkward silence. My dad needed to do something, or maybe he was just worried about the collect phone call.

I knew right then that Isaac would spend the rest of his life dreaming about having been the owner of the IBM building and the Errol Flynn estate. He wasn't going to get me off the street. He couldn't and wasn't really thinking about it.

There was no going back to anywhere I had been before. Those places had disappeared. I would be living my life in parks, beneath bridges or in alleys, or in jail with drunks, Crips, and other home-less. There was nowhere to go back to. My sister and Jean had vanished. It was almost like not having a past. My life was here in Miami Beach. This is where I would likely remain.

~

After the talk with my father, I tossed my broken glasses into the garbage. I realized that looking at the world through the fragment of a broken lens was confusing and dangerous. Sandy was gone, and the glasses were making it impossible for me to see—to really see. I understood this new life was fraught with peril I didn't understand. Focusing on grass and twigs wasn't going to keep me alive.

Living out in the open beneath a tree was too public, too exposed. So I began feeling my way around the park for a new home. Without even a shard of my glasses, the entire world was a blur. I needed to infer information from what I could feel and sense like walking into a dark room and carefully learning what is there. For a couple of days, I searched, returning to my tree at night.

Eventually, in a far corner of the homeless section of the park not far from the canal, I came across a thicket of bushes. When I pushed between them, I found an area of coarse grass and dirt about the size of a small bathroom littered with discarded cans and assorted garbage that had been tossed from the park. This little patch of earth was shielded from other residents of the park and was close enough to the canal so I could feel breeze off the water. It became my new home.

Every day in the park, there were drug deals going down, petty robberies and fights breaking out over women, or because blistering summer heat elicited rage or because folks were half crazy from hunger or despair. Whenever I left my private place, I needed to slip through this homeless world like a ghost or a cat. I trained myself to go unnoticed. I already knew something about this because in my former life I'd spent a year as a candid photographer where drawing attention to oneself was poison to the shoot. But among the homeless, the stakes were higher. When I stepped out of my country retreat, I tried to pretend I was a rabbit hiding in a field, or a statue of a homeless man sitting on a bench with hands in his lap. This is easier to do if you are mostly blind without glasses. If you can't see them, it is easy to fall into the mindset they can't see you, like a child who closes his eyes and believes he can't be seen.

People did their business without noticing or caring I was there. Often residents consummated drug deals while I sat on a bench seemingly in another world. It didn't matter that I was there. I was seen but not seen. I'd sit like this for hours until someone placed a dollar or two in my hand, and then I'd silently slip away to buy cottage cheese and fruit.

I discovered that if you believe you are invisible, you really become invisible. This guise was easier for me to embrace than for others because it was consistent with my identity as an outsider. Also, by now I had lost forty pounds of weight from starvation. In that sense, I was actually becoming invisible. I was feeling more like a spiritual entity, like I was floating through space.

While I was striving to be invisible, there was occasionally a member of the park community who picked up on what I was doing and wanted to talk about it. Approached in this confidential manner, I usually didn't answer. If pressed and my silence seemed to elicit anger, I might respond with a few pleasant words and then move off to another location in the park. Even living invisibly was a balancing act. For some reason that I didn't understand, the non-homeless visitors in the park were much more generous to me when I sat still and silent like an unmoving statue. I think some were attracted to my passivity and wanted to know about my life. Others decided I was partaking in a form of performance art. One afternoon, after I refused to answer his pleasant salutation, a man put a twenty-dollar bill in my hand. I couldn't get over that.

~

In my country home I was eventually accepted by animals as a neighbor. I became especially close with a family of possums. My blandness and passivity won them over. The baby possums were the first to approach me. They were trying to make friends. I began sharing fruit with them. When I arrived from the deli, they ran right over to me and we ate together. When I was asleep at night, the little ones would come and run across my back as if they were playing a game. They were showing off to me or one another, like boys walking across the edge of a wall. Meanwhile, their parents watched from a few feet away. They were pleased their kids were eating my food. It was like living in a community.

When they weren't visiting, the possums lived in the surrounding bushes and trees. All night they made a harmonious clicking chirping sound that became the background of my life. Often, I felt they were communicating with me by the tone of their sounds, which was usually pleasant to listen to, a kind of music. But if a few rats or a stranger began to push his way into the bushes bordering our property, their sound turned harsh and I knew they were issuing a warning. One day their sound was wildly raucous, even alarming, and suddenly a man pushed his way through the bushes holding a gun. He pointed it at my head while the possums screeched in alarm. I stood up and slowly made my way out of my little home and wandered the park for half a day. When I came back in the evening, the stranger had left and the possums were again making their pleasant music.

My friend Fred once told me that old sailors in the Bahamas understand the ocean so well they can navigate without using maps or a compass, just by intuition and looking at subtle signs on the water that fishermen from the city would never notice or understand. They can sense when fish are around while others would just blankly stare at the ocean. Since I was a kid, I've always been attuned to animals, especially cats and birds, and living outdoors in the park, often closed off from other people, these sensitivities deepened. I developed relationships with possums as well as birds. To me, it didn't seem mysterious at all. When I was a kid, I loved my parakeet, and most days I listened to it talk to me. I could sense its mood and I'm sure it could sense mine as well. In the park, I became attuned to the sounds of black birds and feral parrots. At times, they were trying to get my attention. One day I was walking along the sidewalk near the park and the black birds began screeching. I soon noticed they were signaling that a bag of McDonald's food had been dropped into the street. *Please take it off the street and put it on the grass where I can eat it. I can't do it myself.* That's what they were saying to me, and as I came closer to the bag of food, their singing became ecstatic, and when I picked it up, they made a sharp sound. *Yes, yes, yes.* I tossed it onto the grass, and they immediately began picking through the left-over food. Another time I was coming out of the deli near the park when suddenly black birds began bombing me like in an Alfred Hitchcock movie. They wouldn't let me move ahead. I warded them off with my arms. Then they flew off, and a small car came hurtling out of a parking lot across the street, passed in front of me, and smashed through the plate glass window of a store. If I had been moving ahead, the car might have killed me.

~

One morning I woke on the littered plot of grass feeling entirely lost. I didn't know where I was or why I felt this way. I didn't know where to go. My reality was suddenly shattered for no reason I could understand. I stood up from the bed of plastic bags, and took a crap behind a tree.

I stopped thinking for hours.

Then I thought about eating, but I didn't eat a bite. I was hungry but I didn't want to eat.

I had never felt such sorrow. Maybe Branden was right. I was completely crazy. It came on me in a moment. Like losing a close friend I'd never known. I was astounded this had happened to me.

I was embarrassed and terrified. This new vision of myself made me feel like a girl. I tried not to acknowledge it. I felt that if I gave this mood sway, I would become telepathic and I didn't want to know what other people were thinking. I didn't want to know what was in their minds. Because I knew I wouldn't like it. I felt that I needed to protect myself. If I gave myself to this feeling I wouldn't be able to turn it off. So I tried to shield myself. Maybe I could develop a mask of indifference.

For days I didn't eat anything. Long-time park residents started bringing me food each day. They could sense that I was disappearing.

Such grief, unlike anything I'd ever experienced before. All because of the trouble that someone else had. Someone I didn't know. Someone I had never met.

Part V

During the years that my friend Ralph was living in parks and abandoned lots in Florida, I rarely thought about him. Life is that way. The most passionate and seemingly unforgettable moments fall into the past and become replaced by more current memories that feel precious and immutable. Or the good old days become rewritten so they have some connection with the evolving narratives of a life.

When Ralph made his collect calls to me from a phone booth within sight of the Fontainebleau hotel, our conversations became like echoes from a former life or from a fictive life. With time it became harder to know which.

I reminded him of the hamburger-eating contest he'd had with Ronnie Penn who was the star player on our high school basketball team—though much smaller than Ronnie, Ralph had eaten him to a draw, which had delighted me—and the Chinese dinners we'd enjoyed before going off to watch sexy art flicks. I recalled breezy afternoons sailing on the Long Island Sound with my wife and his girlfriend. Jean would always bring along delectable picnic lunches packed in a basket, and a favorite bottle of wine as if we were filming a tv episode celebrating the good life. That was when I was in graduate school at NYU. Soon after, I was teaching English at the College of the Virgin Islands on St. Thomas, and several times Ralph and Jean joined my wife and me on the island. One time, Ralph came to St. Thomas with a folder of carefully drawn engineering plans for the magnetic engine he'd been designing—a motor that did not need gasoline or diesel to power a car. My friend always had a new idea simmering—each of them with the potential to make millions. I didn't understand how he came up with one after the next. I wracked my brains and never thought of a single idea for an invention. We celebrated Ralph's magnetic motor with a pricey steak dinner at the Mafolie Restaurant high in the mountains of St. Thomas. We were all basking in Ralph's glory with an unforgettable view of the night-lights of the harbor while eating steaks and shrimps that were incomparable.

But eventually, the repetition of even the best of old times felt like drudgery. It became hard to summon old laughs we'd once shared. At the first sound of my friend's giggle—same throaty laugh as when we headed off to lusty films or began drumming on our desks while Mr. Fuqua struggled to teach us algebra—I felt impatient or annoyed that Ralph was spending mindless years sitting on a park bench staring at his hands. How could I relate to this? Over the years there were many collect calls. For the most part I went through the motions until I could find an excuse to get off the line. I wasn't thinking about Ralph anymore. I didn't want to think about him.

~

When I was twelve or thirteen and my parents were no longer speaking but were still living together in our house in Great Neck, I started making winter trips with my dad to Miami Beach. We went fishing and spent the week in the Fontainebleau hotel. Those trips with my lighting salesman dad made an indelible mark. I left our home in Great Neck dreaming of catching a hefty kingfish on one of the Miami Beach party boats that left daily from Baker's Haulover Docks about two miles north of the Fontainebleau and not very far from the park where twenty years later my friend Ralph would make his home. I had already decided one day I would own a sport fishing boat and troll those same waters off-shore of the hotels for marlin like Ernest Hemingway.

Most Florida nights, Dad and I went out to dinner at fancy steak restaurants where there was always a table for us no matter how large the crowd lined up at the front door waiting their turn to get inside. The head waiter always gave my dad a warm handshake and made a big show of leading him majestically to an empty table. It only added to his magic when I once noticed my emaciated father slipping the waiter a twenty before the handshake. I loved that slick move that led us through the crowded restaurant to our table and I felt so proud to be his boy. He could

hardly eat more than a few forkfuls in those days because of coli-
tis, so I ate for both of us while he admired my appetite. "Look at
him eat," he'd say proudly to anyone within earshot. I loved that
he bragged about my appetite, that I could do what he couldn't do
anymore. For this boy, Miami Beach was where you went when
you were on top, like me and my dad.

One night in the grand hotel, Dad tucked me into bed and
said he'd be back soon. When I woke at 4:00 a.m., he still hadn't
returned to our room and I knew he was experiencing the sublime
pleasure of this wonderous place, pleasure I could only barely
imagine. I was so excited about his late night adventure, I couldn't
sleep until he came back into our room at dawn.

~

Many years later, I flew to Fort Lauderdale to meet friends for
a few days fishing in the Florida Keys. I arrived a day early so I
could visit Ralph whom I hadn't seen in several years. Ralph said
he would meet me at a deli a couple of miles north of the Fontainebleau Hotel.

But I wasn't thinking about my friend. Old memories were
crowded out by my plans in Florida—I still hadn't decided if we
would fish in the Gulf Stream or cast on the bonefish flats for tarpon,
and I wondered if the Green Turtle Inn still had turtle on the menu.
And I was already missing my feisty little son back in New York.

Probably Ralph wouldn't show up to meet me and that would
be okay, a relief actually. I could no longer picture him or what

we could possibly talk about that would feel fresh and alive. The thought of Ralph living on the street felt so goddamned without purpose. What the hell was he doing with his life? You cannot be a brilliant philosopher and inventor sitting under a tree, can you? Our past was now burdened by years of whoever we had become.

Then I caught sight of the Fontainebleau Hotel in my rearview mirror and pulled my car over to the side on Collins Avenue. Even though the hotel was long past its best days, that curved sweeping shape invoked in me such memories of my father along with youthful fantasies of glamor and forbidden sexuality. For a few minutes, I took in the look of it again and actually considered turning back to the hotel, parking for twenty minutes and hunting around for intimations of my youth, but then thought better of it. Better not to look too closely.

When I arrived in front of the fruit store, there was a man waiting. I would never have recognized him in filthy pants and a tattered safari jacket, face blackened with dirt, a beard halfway down his chest, and long, greasy hair knotted around leaves and twigs.

"Fred, look at us, we're getting so old," he said, referring to our graying hair. We hadn't seen each other in a long time.

I gave him a hug. As a kid, Ralph been a terrible athlete, actually no athlete at all. He had always been pudgy, a softy, but he wasn't soft anymore. He was bone thin and he smelled bad, unbelievably bad.

"Let's have some lunch," I said, thinking of a good deli, the kind we used to go to in the city for nova and bagels.

"I always buy my food here." We went inside and he selected papayas and a grapefruit, explaining that cooked food compromises his beliefs. To my relief, he allowed me to pay. Whenever I offered to send him money from New York, he ended our conversation with a curt "No thanks."

"I want to take you to my home," he said.

We drove a half dozen blocks south on Collins Avenue to a fairly large park with couples walking or seated on the lawn, mothers strolling with curious smiling babies, boys tossing a football pretending to be Dan Marino, until we arrived at a far corner of the park populated exclusively by homeless people sitting on benches or on the grass, not talking or moving much at all. Ralph nodded to a few people he knew and soon we pushed our way through a hedge of rough bushes into an area of scrawny lawn littered with empty beer cans and discarded plastic bags. I noticed a large hunting knife thrust into the trunk of a tree. We sat on the ground, leaning against trees, and from behind one of them came a runty black cat, dragging itself into my friend's lap, mewing for fruit.

Nearby, there was an unkempt bed of plastic bags and a shopping bag of old clothes, which my friend explained he never wore, preferring to live month after month in what he had on, believing that this clothing invested him with the power to survive. I kept eying the army knife plunged into the tree trunk.

"It seems nice here," I said, grasping for something to say.

"Well, there are a lot of animals," he answered.

"What kind of animals?"

"Well, you see the cat and at night possums or rats. I can't be sure what they are in the dark. They crawl on me while I sleep. One of them nipped my finger last night."

He showed me his blacked finger.

"You should get that looked at," I said and then quickly realized such remarks fall into the abyss that separates our two worlds.

I looked around his home trying to appear relaxed. We were both trying to summon something of what once was.

Finally, Ralph asked me about my career, and he nodded seriously as I spoke of my fears of failure—he has always done this—an exaggerated nodding that suggested he was really taking in what I was saying, but I was never really sure about this. Ralph's ideas were always so much bigger than mine. His inventions, of course. And in a lifetime, I could never comprehend the ideas in analytic philosophy he'd developed with Saul Kripke.

Coming up with the next thing to say was unbearable. I managed some recollection about Jean and after another pause Ralph said he'd been feeling regret over never having had children with her. And I was thinking, why couldn't he still have children if a few things fell into place? I guess the big knife thrust into the tree had me feeling edgy. The place felt like a trap and I wanted to get out of there.

"You know, Fred, I was arrested yesterday," Ralph said. "The cops came in here and pulled me out of my bed. They took me to a jail in Miami. I got out this morning and walked back ten miles."

He bit into a grapefruit and sucked on it.

"That's terrible, Ralph," I said, wanting to give him a hug. But I didn't.

~

I wanted to take Ralph to a good restaurant. For some reason, I couldn't think of the name of one I'd visited with my dad, but how could I? That was thirty years ago. We drove south on Collins Avenue until I found a nice-looking steak restaurant. I guess I was trying to pull Ralph into my Miami. Or maybe I was trying to jolt him from the homeless life, or maybe I was just thinking of myself and the old days with my father. I'm not really sure.

A very pleasant hostess looked us over; surely, she had second thoughts about the way Ralph looked and smelled. But the place was mostly empty, and she didn't say anything and led us to a booth in the back of the restaurant. Ralph appraised the elegant place settings and giggled a little. Maybe we both thought it was kind of cool or entirely preposterous that I had brought him to such a place. He told me that he hadn't eaten meat more than several times in the past nine years. But that didn't turn out to be much of a problem. There were plenty of vegetables on the menu. We started with a delicious Caesar salad, and Ralph didn't seem to mind the anchovies. He was famished. I was distracted. Everything I had to say was attached to the past. My mom's abstract paintings, the Siamese cats in our apartment in River-dale, the night he analyzed Dylan Thomas's poetry for me, the guilt I still felt about once hiding his glasses while he searched for them half-blind. He giggled the same way he had in high school. I couldn't pierce his new life. He said a few things but probably I was impatient, and he stopped talking.

So we ate our food and Ralph commented a couple of times that this was a nice restaurant.

I dropped him off at the park during a battering rainstorm. My friend was drenched the moment he stepped out of the car. I watched him walking back into the park in gale force winds and torrential rain. The thought came to me, I should roll down my window and shout out to him, "Ralph, get back into the car and spend the night with me in my motel room." I'd like to say that I shouted this to him, I should have, but I didn't. I watched him dissapear into the park and then drove off.

Part VI

Chinese Food

After months secluded in my tiny home, I came out one day and began to wander around the park. I still wasn't speaking very much, but I had forgotten about being invisible and being mostly blind now felt like an impediment. Being homeless in some respects is like the normal life. We change. We are depressed or happier. What worked before, may no longer work. We learn. We evolve. Someone told me that a nearby library had a box outside the front door that was filled with discarded eyeglasses. I walked there, tried on five or six until I found a pair that mostly worked. I walked back to the park with vision. I sat on a park bench waiting for a handout. I still could not bring myself to beg for money—that still seemed disgusting to me—but I was happy to take whatever was offered. Increasingly I chatted with residents of the park. My old friend Sandy had returned from her travels. I asked about her life and she told me she had visited her aging parents in their lavish estate in

Connecticut, had tooled around back roads in their new Mercedes. It would all be hers one day—she wanted me to know this—but finally she couldn't bear her parents and had returned to Florida and her boyfriend in his big condo on the beach. I guessed this was Sandy's fantasy because she was usually among the homeless in the park, but I was never sure about this.

To survive years in the street or a park or under a bridge, one must absorb the mores and etiquette of the life. Residents of the park cooperate in small ways. If there is something I can do that is helpful, I should do it. "Can you watch my bag? I'll be back in a half hour." "Sure." Small favors and kindnesses form associations. Clumps of people hang together until some wander off. We are no longer strangers, but not exactly friends. You can't count on anything. There is no such thing as for sure. There is no such thing as money in the bank. But maybe you can have some change in your pocket.

There are long stretches of time where nothing happens and you feel like nothing ever will. The boredom feels eternal. Then nearby two men begin to argue. One of them is a martial artist with a face disfigured from a bullet wound. Sitting beside him is a smaller man, a tough Puerto Rican who is talking in a harassing way. I am sitting nearby. They seem on the verge of battle. I want to stand up and run for my life. But I can't leave. It would make me appear weak. If I were to run, they might chase me. I try to watch the birds in the trees while they make dire threats. The boredom of the outdoor life is punctuated by fearful moments.

A lot of younger guys are fighters and are looking for occasions to prove themselves. Most days there are arguments and often fights, but by and large park elders are respected and are exempt from park violence. It is considered dishonorable for a man to strike a woman or to attack an elder.

One day, for no apparent reason, a big black guy sucker-punched a bearded gray-haired elder who spent most days sitting alone on a bench. This older man rarely spoke, never bothered anyone. He was harmless. Why did this happen? It was just the life in this place. A couple of days later, strangers turned up in the park. I never learned where they came from, who called them, or where they took the black guy. We eventually heard that he was left dead on the street.

~

There was an older woman, Juliette, who spent an hour or two each afternoon circling the park at a rapid pace. She was a striking figure, tall, austere, gray-haired. Her bearing was regal while she moved along taking in the view of the park and canal as though strolling the most beautiful sections of Paris. She radiated confidence and style. When she approached, residents gave way to her as if in a former life she had been royalty. Or she was still royalty. She seemed to own it.

Juliette was drawn to me. I have no idea why. Even before we began to talk, if you would call it that, she seemed to be sensing or signaling to me as she came by. Then one day, she sat beside me on a bench and began to speak in a language all her own. I could feel Juliette's mood and often make out what she was saying to me, but to others listening she was talking incomprehensible gibberish. After a while, I understood her language completely or felt that I did. In the park, Juliette was a loner, but to me she poured out her heart. She rued the loss of her small country house in Nyack, and the parties she had once attended in elegant apartments overlooking the Hudson and Central Park, the great painters she had known, friends of her father who was an accomplished painter of military figures. She had once had investments, money funds, and routing numbers. Now she owned nothing. Almost nothing, a few duffel bags grown dusty in a church basement. Telling me about her life and loves, she became emotional and I tried my best to console her.

How, you might ask, could you understand Juliette's talk that sounded like so much noise and nonsense? I don't know exactly, but for starters you must open yourself to feel deeply. It's how one gets along with cats and dogs and lizards. It's how Jean and I shared intimate moments. It's impossible if you don't believe. After a week or two I could usually understand everything Juliette said.

Sandy made it a point to stop by and listen to our afternoon talks. She didn't understand but she could feel the emotion of our connection. She wanted so badly to understand, but she couldn't get through the door. Sandy began to refer to me as a psychiatrist. Soon, my afternoon talks with Juliette became something of a park event.

How do you understand her? I was asked this again and again.

In a jumble of sounds Juliette asked me pointed questions about my life and the unusual path that led me to this park. She believed we were kindred spirits. I don't know about that. But we had much in common. We'd both lost a lot. I, too, had never fit in. Since I was a kid, I'd known I was different. But I'd learned how to fake it better than Juliette. And she was fiercer than I was. She seemed to feel sorrow for me that I didn't feel for myself.

Other park residents who had known me for months or longer now wanted to talk. I was sought out by men and women suffering years of depression, alcoholism, or drug addiction, inmates right out of jail asking me to look at rap sheets and write letters to the Department of Justice citing errors. Many who came to me wanted answers to big questions, most were looking for the magic ticket off the street, but not all wanted to escape this life.

One afternoon, I was walking to the john when a hefty guy came flying out the bathroom door almost knocking me over. A huge white southerner had picked this man up over his head and tossed him through the door like he was a bowling ball. The smaller man, who was not very small, got up off the ground and shrugged like it was just another day in the office.

In time I got to know him quite well. In the late afternoon, he waited for me to show up at the bench where I usually met people. He sat beside me and talked about his life. I quickly came to real- ize for this fellow I wasn't a real flesh-and-blood person, and he wasn't a "normal" homeless man living in the park. Rather, the life we were all living here was a video game where there is only one real person who is a kind of superhero, him. The others in the park were minor characters in the game. I caught on quickly that he didn't believe that other people really exist. To him, I was the wise man in his game of life in the park. To finally win the game, he must take over the parks and back alleys in Miami Beach and become ruler of the streets.

The man's father lived in Bal Harbor, not too far from the park. Once every month or so, he'd show up in our park looking for his son and beg him to come home. But he wouldn't go home with his father. He ridiculed the suggestion, laughed in his father's face. His dad was outside the boundaries of the game that had become the son's life.

I once said to him, all the homeless people here have no place to go. You have a nice home to go back to. Go home. He laughed at this suggestion. It was irrelevant. I was just some character in the game he was playing. I was creating an obstacle for him that he needed to move past.

After a while, I stopped making any suggestions. I just listened, nodded at his vision of the world, let him talk which seemed to please him and calm him down.

~

Once a month my friend Juliette got a small social security check and blew it in one fierce weekend of spending. Two or three times she took me along. We dined in posh restaurants in Palm Beach. We strolled through high-end malls and visited beautiful neighborhoods as if she were a hungry home buyer hunting for the finest area to settle. Juliette wanted to show me how she'd once lived. We stayed in an expensive motel and talked late into the night. I tried to make love to her, but she wouldn't allow that. Maybe she thought I wouldn't enjoy her old body.

During these weekends Juliette spent money as if it were limitless. We gorged on good food. She bought clothes for herself and offered to buy me new outfits, but I declined. She only stopped spending when she still had just enough money left for bus fare back to our park in Miami Beach.

One day, we went to a super fancy mall in Palm Beach. There was a Saks Fifth Avenue there. We checked it out through an outside window in the mall. That month, Saks was featuring ripped blue jeans for $175 and a badly torn blouse for $125. We both started laughing. The homeless look had become the latest style. I never imagined we'd go inside, but Juliette marched right in, and I followed reluctantly.

We rode the escalators upstairs. She seemed to know exactly where she was going. I trailed behind only barely able keep her in sight. Juliette walked confidently ahead as though she owned the place. I was glancing around, waiting for a floor manager to hustle over and throw us out. It felt ridiculous to be here. I was dressed in filthy rags. I hadn't washed myself in weeks. But Juliette moved ahead like a Vanderbilt. We walked through acres of fine clothes heading toward the back of the third floor where dresses went for a thousand dollars; and beyond these fine clothes, at the very back wall of this floor of floors, there was a special boutique area for the wealthiest ladies in the state, custom clothing that cost three times more than anything else in Saks. This was where my friend wanted to be. While she carefully assessed the best of the best, I was thinking they are going to call the police and lock us up. If we were lucky, they'd just toss us out of the store. I was trying to be invisible, but I'd lost the knack for disappearing, and I could see people staring at me. But not her. Somehow Juliette fit right in here.

Now Juliette was deep into conversation with the manager of the boutique. The manager was nodding her head as if taking in sage advice, and when I drew closer still, I heard my friend describing what she was looking for in an evening dress. Juliette was speaking to the lady in near perfect English. I'd known her for a year and had never heard her speak like this. How was this possible? I guess after years in the street living with bums she'd forgotten who she was. Really, it took my breath away.

After returning from this trip, Juliette and I stopped meeting together on the bench. Once or twice I came across her while she circled the park, and we greeted warmly. Soon after this she left the park and I never saw her again. That's how it was here. Friendships were not exactly friendships. I didn't think much about her after this.

~

Over the years, there were many homeless men and women who joined me on the bench for a chat. I'd become known here as a counselor. While I was speaking or listening, usually two or three others were on a nearby bench waiting their turn. "Tell me about yourself," I'd begin. "Why do you say this? Tell me more. What kind of work did you do before you began living on the street?" To be honest, I didn't really know what I was doing. I was faking it. But park residents were fascinated that someone was asking questions about their lives and seemed to care about their sorrows. In the homeless world, everyone is using everybody else to gain an edge. People in the park came to talk to me because they couldn't talk to anyone else. I learned early on that you must take these conversations completely seriously. Even if the person to whom I spoke was barely literate, I needed to apply my intelligence as if working on model logic with Saul Kripke. If you only half-listen or brush them off, they know it. If you patronize them, you can get in trouble or you can get them in trouble.

The most curious thing about counseling fellow residents is that the ones I seemed to help the most eventually developed rancor and distaste for me. They reached a point where they didn't want to look at me anymore or hear the sound of my voice. They now knew better. *You're just some bum I talked to. I'll soon be leaving this place and you'll still be here panhandling and sleeping in the rain.*

Over the years there was a tall, lanky guy from a small town in Ohio, Jim, who came by my bench to talk. I could tell right off Jim felt superior to others living in the park. He looked at me as if to say, I know that you and I don't belong here. Many park residents felt this way but for Jim this was a guiding star.

Jim had been a high school basketball hero. He had made

winning shots in big games. He'd been coveted by the prettiest girls in school. If he'd been able to go to college, he could have been an All-American. And then a pro. He believed this. After he graduated high school, he became a party planner. He arranged some really big parties. "Tell me about them, Jim." He shook his head, no, and fell into silence. He didn't want to think about the parties he'd arranged. Or his troubled relationship with his father. He was baffled about what had happened to him. "How am I here?" He did not want to adapt. He was still living his basketball days, revisiting his winning shots. He could still recall each of them perfectly. Jim was trying to stay adrift on a perfectly placid lake.

In our talks, I tried to convey the attitude it's okay to be a bum. I had the conviction he'd need to live here and now before he could live a life somewhere else. I'd say things like, "If you can be open to it, you can learn from a homeless life." He'd nod as if I were getting through to him, but I never really knew what Jim believed. He didn't want to let too much in and was hard to read.

One day a new guy turned up in the park and came over to us when we were chatting. The new fellow referred to himself as "a homeless person such as myself." While describing his recent street life, he used this phrase over and again. He spoke of the three of us as "homeless people such as ourselves" as if we were tenured college professors having a chat on the lawn between classes. It made my skin crawl. Finally I turned to the guy and said, "We just call ourselves bums." At this Jim started to laugh.

~

One day Jim and I were walking around Miami Beach. Neither of us had eaten a morsel in two days. We passed a Chinese restaurant that was packed. The smell wafting from the open door had me drooling. "I'll bet the food here is delicious," I said.

"I've never eaten Chinese food," Jim said.

"Really?"

It's amazing how we change. At Branden's years earlier, this food would have disgusted me, but now I couldn't imagine anything more appetizing. That's when I noticed a huge garbage bin in the alley alongside the restaurant. It was almost as large as a subway car. But the lip of the bin was eight feet above the ground. You couldn't begin to see what was inside the bin. Maybe nothing of value. Maybe rats. Neither of us had ever eaten garbage before. But the smell of pork dumplings drifting from an open door to the kitchen was indescribable. Anyhow, this mammoth garbage bin was inaccessible.

"But if we could somehow get inside there, we might find some great food," I said to him.

"I've never eaten Chinese food," Jim repeated.

"You might love it."

He didn't seem to believe me. He had serious restraint even though we were both starved.

I pondered the bin. I really had no idea how to manage this. It didn't seem possible.

"We need to find a box, maybe a cardboard box," I said.

Jim didn't want Chinese food, he seemed afraid of it but he had a military mentality. I was the counselor in the park. I was the officer. He was the enlisted man. He trailed me down the block until we came to a liquor store where there were boxes piled outside. I selected one and we headed back to the Chinese restaurant. People were streaming out of the place talking about how good the dumplings are.

"If we can get in there, we'll get some good food."

But now standing right next to the garbage bin, the lip was almost three feet over my head. "I'll never be able to get up there."

Jim looked at the height of the bin and shrugged.

"We've got to find a cinder block," I said, glancing down the alley.

"Maybe standing on the cinder block one of us could manage it."

We were standing right beside the thing. It was towering.

"I don't need any cinder block," Jim said. "You hand me the box when I'm inside."

Jim suddenly levitated up and into the bin, up and in there so fast I couldn't believe my eyes. How'd he do that? Now Jim had his hand up waiting for me to toss the cardboard box. For the next five or ten minutes, I waited while Jim rustled around inside the garbage bin. It's hard to judge time when your heart is pounding from hunger and worry the police are going to come racing down the alley. Finally, Jim emerged from the lip of the bin dripping with chow mein and lobster sauce, and he carefully handed the box down to me.

It was about half a mile hike back to the park in the heat of midday, and all the while I was afraid the cops were going to pick us up. I'd never robbed food before. Jim carried the box. He was a strong guy. After a while, he began taking things out and feeding them to me with his fingers, a sparerib, a chicken wing, a piece of egg roll. He wanted to make sure he wasn't going to get poisoned.

I was eating everything he handed me. It was good fresh food. I always liked Chinese food until I started hating it. Eventually Jim reached in and grabbed a lobster tail and devoured it.

~

Hunting for food in dumpsters became a significant part of my life. I learned that being successful is like being a good fisherman or hunter, learning the best times to go out looking, where to go, and what to look out for. There is a time of day when different restaurants around town put out the food. You want to be there right after workers have finished dumping the refuse of a heavy lunch or dinner, when the food is still unspoiled by rats, or from the sun and baking heat of Miami. You want to arrive at a time when local police are less likely to be around. I soon developed an intuitive feel for when to go to the Chinese place on Collins Avenue or an Italian restaurant across town that had delicious clam sauce or a steak house where they served excellent roast beef.

The park people who regularly hit dumpsters are very good at what they do, and the very best are artists. Jim was no artist but he was passably okay. He was a good leaper, but he was messy as hell, had no sense for the food he shoveled into the box and worst of all he had no feel for danger.

After six months or so, Jim and I were only rarely having chat sessions on the bench, and when we did speak, he no longer mentioned his basketball life. I felt good about that although I knew we were reaching the end of the line. I had become the officer Jim could no longer tolerate.

Jim and I went hunting for dumpster food together six or eight times and that was that. When I heard he was hitting dumpsters with another park resident, I cautioned him to check with me before going back to the Chinese restaurant on Collins. That monster dumpster was inviting as hell, but the police were often patrolling the neighborhood. Jim didn't listen. I knew he wouldn't. He went there with the other guy, leaped in without a care, and they were both picked up by the cops and spent two weeks in jail. That was the best dumpster in Miami Beach, but we could never go back there again. The owners were now closely watching it.

Soon after Jim got out of jail, he stopped by the park for a few nights and then disappeared, forever I figured. But I was wrong about this. About a year later, I was walking along A1A and I noticed a slick car, a Buick Riviera I think, stopped at a red light. When I came a little closer, I saw it was Jim driving with his elbow leaning out the window like Don Johnson in *Miami Vice*. I approached the car and he didn't notice me at first. Then I came right up to his window like any bum on the street. "Mister, can you spare a quarter?" That was my joke because Jim knew from before I never panhandled. Jim took a good look at me, nodded one time, and drove off without a word. Okay, I felt a twinge of pain but mostly the encounter left me feeling good.

For the majority of park residents I tried to help my message was, the best thing you can do for yourself is get off the street and stay off. The more successful they were at this, the more successful I felt.

Part VII

The years passed. Ralph and I spoke only very occasionally when he was in a phone booth after being unable to reach his dad. We didn't have much to talk about anymore and hadn't for years. I'd stopped bringing up the high school days in Riverdale. Ralph had never been much for nostalgia, but one or the other of us would usually ask, how have you been? A question nearly as absurd to both of us as asking about the weekend weather on the moon. Neither of us tried hard on these calls, which was frankly a relief to us both.

One time though, Ralph happened to call during a span of weeks when his father had been phoning me repeatedly to ask a favor. Isaac had read one of my articles in *New York Magazine* and decided I could help him get his buildings back. He had been planning to countersue the state of New York for suing him for back taxes. He felt sure that if I wrote an article exposing the government for unfair treatment, he'd surely win his lawsuit and would soon be back in the building business. I told him that I didn't know if my editor would allow me to write such a piece, but I'd think about it. Isaac didn't want to hear maybes. "You can do this for your friend Ralph. Then he'll be a rich man. Don't you want to help Ralph?" Ralph was laughing like the old days while I described trying to reason with his dad. Isaac wouldn't let me get off the phone until I promised to seriously consider writing the article about his buildings. "If not for *New York Magazine*, then write it for another magazine. Write it for Ralph." Then a week later, he called again to start the same discussion.

At the end of one of Isaac's calls, I inquired about his second family living in Rye. He said almost casually, that several years earlier, his oldest son had burned down the main house, and the last he'd heard they were all living in a cramped apartment above the garage. He didn't seem to know more about his second family than this. They weren't on his mind. He wanted to win back his buildings. This news about the Errol Flynn house elicited another giggle from Ralph who thanked me for the update and that was that. He had moved on.

I felt jarred by this phone call. Ralph had slammed the door on everything that had come before. His father, of course, but also on our friendship long ago in New York, the thrilling late-night talks about mutability, nova and bagels before Sunday football. What secret treasure had Ralph discovered that kept him on the street? I didn't get it. All the time he'd been gone, whenever I thought about him, I wanted to pull him back. As if the many years had been a fanciful interlude, a fling. I'd never imagined he wouldn't want to come back.

~

Sometime later, on a sunny Sunday afternoon, I walked to Washington Square Park, about six blocks from my apartment in Soho. I'd come looking for happy music, drumming, "Hare Krishna" singers, maybe a jazz band, but there was no music on this day. Probably the police had shut down the music because of complaints from the wealthy who lived in town houses bordering the park. Bad luck for me. I'd come on the day the music stopped.

I was about to walk back home to watch a football game with my wife and little boy, when I noticed a skinny, elderly black lady in soiled clothes walking from the southwest corner of the park where chess hustlers played into the night. Leaning on her hip was a black man who seemed to have crossed into a different realm. She was walking toward my usual bench near the fountain in the center of the park with the man hanging on her, mumbling and moaning. She was remarkably strong and carried her burden with stature and grace. I was immediately drawn to her, wanted to know about her life or at least hear her voice. But she passed by my bench without a glance and then veered to the left heading for the northwest section of the park where the benches were occupied exclusively by homeless in various states of filth and undress. The lady was grimy from the street but beautiful, and I guessed, kind and nurturing. As she dragged the man ahead, others in this community turned to watch the agitated man for a few moments and then fell back into their own musings. I couldn't take my eyes off her. She was talking quietly, saying caring words I imagined, as she dragged him along. She found an empty bench where she deposited the man who immediately began shouting in tongues, spitting saliva, kicking his feet, convulsing. She left him on the bench and retired to another bench a hundred feet away and sat with several homeless men as if she'd done all that she could and that was that.

All the benches in this section of the park were occupied by homeless people as best I could tell. The ones nearby turned to watch the convulsing man for a few moments and then fell back into their own solitude.

I watched for the next ten minutes as the man writhed, called out, and for some reason pulled his pants down to his knees. The lady never turned back to look at him. Finally I got up and walked toward her. I wasn't sure what was the best way to introduce myself. Perhaps I would speak about my homeless friend in Miami Beach. As a journalist, I am practiced at meeting strangers and seeing where the conversation leads. As I approached their bench, one of the men sitting beside her fell onto the asphalt on all fours searching for something, maybe a shard of a cigarette or joint. He couldn't find it and sat back beside the lady. I was standing in front of her about to introduce myself when she said to me, "You don't belong here."

Part VIII

There was one night I will never forget. A large gazebo in the center of our Miami Beach park was often used for chamber music concerts with high-end musicians playing on a raised platform and hundreds of music lovers sitting on the lawn savoring Chopin, Schubert, or Tchaikovsky in the evening breeze coming off the Intracoastal. But on this night the gazebo was unpopulated and without any plan or forethought of consequences the homeless of our park gathered on the gazebo, we invaded it you might say, and we started smoking weed and someone brought a boom box and soon everyone was slow dancing to soul music. We didn't care about the law or what passersby were thinking of us. Not then. We were like folks in a small town caring about one another, at least on this lovely breezy evening. We didn't have a dollar but there was a transcendent feeling, a bond of the desperate, of people who have lost everything.

I noticed at the edge of our group a very short Asian woman I'd never seen before. She danced in her own world, her face obscured by long, lustrous black hair. Her bare feet were filthy and her dance at times was ugly and awkward, as if she felt defiled, but then she would bloom like a flower and her posture opened and became beautiful and welcoming. I couldn't take my eyes off her. Her dance seemed to tell the story of a lost life and a great wealth of art and beauty locked deep inside.

Then all at once, people on the gazebo started laughing, laughing without restraint, souls at the end of their ropes with no future, didn't know what they will eat tonight or where to stay dry in the fierce squalls that roll in most evenings. But we were alive, we are real, and at least among ourselves we are significant, even though we have nothing. And that's what we were laughing about! A weird euphoria of the homeless and the dispossessed.

~

But during these several months in my many years of homeless life, there was a break from hunger. Several of us were going out to restaurants bringing back boxes of really delicious food to share with park residents.

As I mentioned earlier, the best hunters of garbage containers were artists. But there was no one I ever worked with who could match David's grace and feel for working a trash dumpster.

The night he first appeared in our park, David was all beat up. He'd been living by railroad tracks to the west and had been left for dead by some homeless thugs. A few of us fed him and looked out for him while he healed. I asked him to tell me how he had once made a living and he shook his head no. He wouldn't talk about his past at all. He wouldn't even tell me his last name. Never did. He didn't trust white people. He slowly got stronger and stronger. Finally one night he asked if I wanted to go with him to find some food.

I am a short man and even as a kid, I could barely jump. Only once or twice as I recall, did I manage to climb into an unusually short garbage dumpster myself. It's so much easier if you are an athlete, a leaper. You don't need to drag any cinder blocks half a block. Easy in and easy out. It was always my job to decide what restaurants to hit, then to stand outside the dumpster holding a cardboard box ready to hand it up while looking out for police.

Without forethought or hesitation or need for a cinder block, David levitated into the highest bins. He jumped and climbed like a sherpa. Sometimes the conditions were far from perfect, no light at all with food all mixed up, yesterday's moldy lunch specials mixed in with dinners that were still warm and savory. On a moonless night in a dark alley, David could feel with his fingers what was fresh, fairly fresh, or too foul to take.

As often as I witnessed his approach, I never understood how he did it. David could see with his hands. He knew what to put in the box from a massive, mixed-up garbage bin and what to leave for the rats. He worked his way through the largest dumpster without getting dirty. Jim had always come out of a dumpster matted with grease and soy sauce, but David never got dirty once that I saw. He bounded out of the bin clean as he went in. This always amazed me.

Before he left our park for some other homeless place, David and I hit a lot of dumpsters together. We rarely talked but we enjoyed walking around Miami Beach, savoring the change of seasons and beautiful ladies on the beach while discovering new restaurants to sample. I once told him that our friendship reminded me of the Billy Joel song. "Yes, they're sharing a drink they call loneliness. But it's better than drinkin' alone."

David smiled when I told him this.

~

One late afternoon as I was chatting with a park regular, I noticed the Asian lady whom I had watched dancing in the gazebo sitting on the bench beside mine, as if waiting her turn. I was flustered when she came over to me and gestured if it was okay to sit beside me. She wanted to talk. I couldn't imagine what to say to this unusual stranger. I didn't know how to begin.

Speaking with her was a different challenge than learning to understand Juliette or even a possum. Mandarin Chinese was like trying to penetrate a wall. We began with gestures, hers and mine, though her gestures were much more nuanced than my own. She had small hands and the face of a beautiful twelve-year-old girl. Straining to understand, I felt old and ungainly.

"Okay," I said, "You've come from China." She nodded yes. "You had something very small but it's gone." She shook her head no, no. Her gestures were much more subtle than mine. She could practically speak with her body. I should have been able to understand her more easily, but I was thrown off by her otherworldly manner. Also, I felt uneasy because some of my regular "clients" were watching and wondering. "Oh, you had a baby. But she is gone." No, no, no. She shakes her head. She holds a baby or small child in her arms, rocks her, smiles. "You miss her so much." Again, she shakes her head no, a little sadly. I feel like a dolt. Why can't I understand? Why? She had me twisted all around. Not only did she speak in Mandarin, but she spoke in riddles.

She came closer to me and seemed to uncover the face of a baby or a small child so that I could see. "This is your baby? You are holding her now in your arms?" I venture. She nods yes, further uncovering an imaginary face so there could be no doubt. "She is really beautiful," I say hopefully. She nods. She almost cries. She loves her so much and her joy is infectious.

Jenny took my hand and seemed to lead me to her meaning. Hints. Many unusual hints. She was arrestingly artful with her hands and body. Jenny had a secret world. If someone will allow you into one corner of a secret world, then you can build on that slowly, carefully, one revelation at a time. You get moving on a track. The raising of an eyebrow. "Yes, I understand now." A small smile. A word that symbolizes a whole world of things. A lot of laughter. Her laugh is infectious. She is so pleased that we understand each other.

We talked together, sort of, for two hours. At times she appeared hopeless, pathetic, and then something spurred joy and as in her dance on the gazebo she became achingly beautiful—I could barely look at her then. Here is what she told me the first afternoon.

I am a single mother. I gave birth to my baby in China. My baby's father has another family. When his wife found out about me, I left China because I didn't want to damage his family. In America I have been living on the streets or in parks like this one. I have been able to make a little money to eat and feed my daughter by dancing in parks.

But in truth, Jenny might have said almost anything to me and I would have been enchanted. Just sitting with her was such an unusual and intense pleasure. Almost overnight I felt she had changed my life. I kept thinking that she would stand up, move away from my bench and I'd never see her again.

We were noticed. Our park community was small and the homeless gossip like everyone else. I tried to shut that out. I didn't want her to disappear as quickly as she had walked into my sorrowful life.

For the next three days, Jenny met me in the afternoon on the bench to chat. But during these wonderous afternoons, my dialogues with other homeless souls withered. My clients didn't want to talk about their grief or to develop a plan of escape from the streets, and frankly I had lost interest in these dialogues. They wanted to know about the girl and some asked me questions. The connection I had with Jenny, tenuous as it was, had aroused appetites. I hardly knew what to say to men I had been speaking with for months. They had come to me for answers. But now I

119

was entirely distracted, passing time until she again settled on the bench beside me. If she came again. Would she come again? I only thought about Jenny.

On the fourth or fifth day of Jenny's visits, I managed to slowly translate this from her expressions, gestures, and small windows of epiphany.

I had a dream that I was still living in China, waiting for a bus, and I met a tall black woman who was wearing a red hat. She surprised me when she began speaking perfect Mandarin. While we waited for the bus, she told me that she had grown up in Africa and that her father was leading a revolution of the oppressed. He had sent her away to China to be safe from the coming war.

Needless to say, at first, I didn't know what to make of this dream or why she told it to me. But as we sat together quietly in the darkening afternoon, I sensed that Jenny identified me with the father of the black lady in her dream, a leader of the oppressed. I asked her why she thought this and she smiled. Nothing more.

Later that night as I was falling asleep, I heard someone gently pushing the bushes aside followed by the cacophony of the possums who guarded our little world of crab grass and tossed garbage.

As soon as Jenny entered our little space, the possums quieted down as if sensing that all was well. She sat next to me on the ratty lawn and said with gestures that she and her daughter were afraid in the park, especially on a moonless night. She asked if she could sleep in this more protected place with me. She promised that her daughter would not keep me awake, she was a very quiet little girl. I nodded yes and without another word, she put her head on a parcel of old clothing I handed to her, brought her child into her arms, and fell asleep to the music of the night birds and possums.

It was a perfectly innocent night, lovely and restful, but next morning in the park the change was cataclysmic.

~

In the street life, the only real law is power and brute physical dominance. The rules, such as they are, are refuse from an earlier time. There is no leadership to speak of. As an elder and counselor, I seemed to have a sliver of leadership, but I had no illusions.

I felt the snickering remarks each time Jenny and I chatted on a bench. I realized almost immediately once you have an attractive young girl, someone here will move in on you. There is nothing to stop this from happening. After spending our first night together, I was no longer a respected elder, just another sixty-five-year-old bum. I didn't have a dollar, but I was suddenly the keeper of a different kind of wealth. Many of the young men here had been in jail for violent or sexual offenses. Any one of them might do anything to her or to me. Even innocuous guys posed a threat—I don't want to take this guy's girlfriend away, but someone's going do it so I might as well. Here, you move in on the things you want. You just take it.

One afternoon I came out from the bathroom, and a young man with tattoos all over his heavily muscled arms and shoulders was sitting beside her, making his case. She looked very uncomfortable. I imagined he was saying to her, "You don't need that old piece of shit." I worried that he would take her by the arm and pull her to a far corner of the park or to another park. I would never see her again. Jenny was wrong. I am not a leader of the oppressed. No one answers to anyone here, and surely not to me. If this guy leads her away, there is nothing I can do—he could kill me in a minute. But for some reason he walks off, leaves Jenny alone . . . until tomorrow. Or the day after. I can't protect her. I can't protect myself. I survived on the streets for years being a ghost. I could not be a ghost with Jenny beside me.

The next night we were lying together on plastic bags, the three of us, in our little retreat, heads resting on bags of old clothes. I told her that it has become very dangerous here. She was already learning to understand me, but I was talking way too fast for her. I needed to force myself to slow down, but it felt like we were being chased by dogs. She asked with her eyes, what can we do. I felt awful that I had scared her. I answered slowly with gestures and a few words that we should leave here in the morning. Travel to the north where there are places that are safer for both of us to live. I worried that she would say no. Why would she ever go away with me. She hardly knows me. But she nodded yes without a hesitation. She seemed to believe in me. She fell asleep holding her little girl. It's uncanny how quickly my life had changed.

In the morning, Jenny and I took stock of our finances. I had two dollars and some change. Knotted in a rag, she had seven dollars in change saved from her dancing. That's what we had to start a new life. We gathered our few things in plastic bags and two battered duffels. Jenny held her little girl in her arms, spoke to her quietly, while I carried the bags and walked out of the park that had been my home for many years. I never turned to take a last glance. We were a dystopian couple setting out for a safer place to start again.

I'd heard rumors there were a few homeless communities to the north, around Pompano Beach. I recalled some bum saying Pompano had a friendly small-town atmosphere, the local police weren't so fast to haul you in. But honestly, I was hoping and guessing about Pompano, and for some reason I liked the name. We walked a mile or so to a bridge crossing the Intracoastal to Biscayne Boulevard. We waited there for a northbound bus. After ten or fifteen minutes, a bus came into view, slowed down to a crawl as it approached our stop. The driver took a glance our way and kept going. After standing a half hour in the sun, a bus stopped for us. The driver didn't look happy when I stumbled aboard in my blackened safari jacket hauling our pathetic luggage. I looked for two seats that were separated by a couple of rows from other passengers. Venturing into the world from the street you are always self-conscious about the way you look and smell.

Except for a couple of trips with Juliette, this was the first traveling I'd done in twenty years. Expensive homes were soon flashing past, slick dressers speeding by in luxury cars, folks who never worried about a big meal or a glass of clean water. As we headed north, I was grooving on a movie I'd watched long ago. The things people take for granted that I'd almost forgotten. I had once lived like the guys driving the highways to fancy homes and apartments.

Then I looked over at Jenny talking to her kid and for a moment the sight of her was jolting. She had actually come with me for this outlandish trip to God knows where we were going and what the hell would become of us. So young and otherworldly. How could this work? She didn't seem to notice the houses with boats in the backyards or the lavish cars. What did she know? Where did she come from? What did she want? I knew nothing about Jenny who had put her life in my hands. I really didn't get it. I didn't want to disappoint her. I was just an old bum. I was way past having big dreams. This responsibility weighed on me as we headed north.

At Broward Terminal, we switched to a number 10 bus into Pompano. I was afraid we wouldn't have the money to make it all the way but the fare ended up costing three dollars for each of us.

Finally the driver stopped somewhere on Federal Highway and pointed to the east, that's where we'd find the beach. The late-afternoon sun was battering. We weren't dressed for such heat. I always wore my safari jacket believing it kept me alive. Jenny wore a tanned full-length skirt stained from sleeping on the ground. We were soon drenched with sweat beneath our clothes. What a risk we were taking leaving Miami Beach where we knew how to eat and sleep. It amazed me that she kept walking beside me as if I knew where we were going. We passed neat little offices and then a big Winn-Dixie. Eventually we passed a park. Jenny looked over at me as a question, should we go in there, take a rest. I shook my head as if I knew our Valhalla was to the east. But really this was crazy because I was faking it. About then, a shout from the park now behind us, "Ralph, Ralph . . . What you doing here?" I was stunned by this. A guy I knew from the park in Miami Beach was waving at me. I guess I was afraid if I stopped now, we'd settle into this park and basically we'd have traveled here to substitute one park of bums for another. I gave him a long wave and we kept walking.

I learned in subsequent days there were a lot of homeless in Pompano, living in parks, in vacant lots, behind buildings and in alleys. You notice them from time to time, looking around, looking you over, but mainly keeping to their friends, folks barely hanging onto the edge of the world.

Jenny said to me her baby was hungry and she was trying to comfort her. Where the hell was the beach? I had a feeling we must be getting close. In front of a Grand Union, there was a hot dog stand, and I bought us two with sauerkraut along with one soda to share. After another half hour walking, we came to a convenience store and I pulled her inside. Jenny didn't have much left. I quickly found a bound yellow pad and a couple of pencils and as I paid for them she looked at me in disbelief, made me shiver. We were down to our last dollar. That was it. But somehow, in my mind, so much depended on this yellow pad and the pencils. I was sure it was what we needed most.

Jenny and her little girl were too tired to go on. What I would have given for a clean room to spend the night, take showers, and have a good meal. But I had nothing to give. I thought of my dad's old office buildings. We'd had all sorts of money to burn on a thousand whims a month. I wanted to give her some hope, but I couldn't think of a thing to say. What a fool I had been. We shouldn't have left Miami until we'd collected more money. I kept thinking she would walk away and I'd never see her again.

By now, I was half-dragging her. I didn't know how much further to the beach, and then what? We passed a sprawling building with a string of doctor and dentist offices locked for the night. Outside the offices, there was a long breezeway, and part of it was mostly obscured from the sidewalk by a row of benches. I led her to a spot behind the benches. "Rest here with your daughter," I said, and rushed back down the block to the Grand Union. Behind it, there was a garbage bin, and alongside there was a big pile of corrugated delivery boxes. I grabbed several of them and carried them back to the breezeway. I spread them out on the planked wooden floor, and before I could even pull out some old clothes for her to rest her head, Jenny was asleep clutching her little girl on the cardboard behind the benches.

In the cool of morning, it was an easy walk along Atlantic Avenue to the beach. From two blocks away, I saw a large white sign, Welcome to Pompano Beach. I felt like it was speaking to me, to us.

When we drew near, the place was already alive with eighty or a hundred men, women, kids, and old-timers with fishing rods and handlines and buckets of bait making their way out toward the end of the pier that extended eight hundred feet into the ocean. A handful of regulars brought several fishing rods to use simultaneously increasing their odds. Such guys live and die for these hours on the pier. These were mostly working people or elderly and even some homeless who could never once in a lifetime afford to troll the Gulf Stream right offshore of this pier on fancy thousand-dollar-a-day sportfishing boats. But dropping a line off this pier, if luck was with you, you could pull a kingfish up on the dock or a shark, or if you had a day of days, even sailfish or a yellowfin tuna. This was a place where a regular guy or even a homeless guy could make the catch of a millionaire. The air was clear here, and the evening ocean breeze was as invigorating as off St. Thomas or Tahiti. I knew immediately this would be our new home.

I didn't tell Jenny right then what I had in mind. She sat on a bench at the foot of the pier and seemed happy feeling the easterly breeze off the ocean, her eyes half-closed, while holding her little girl in a light blanket to protect her from the sun. There was a res-taurant across from where she was seated and the smell of food on the grill was irresistible, but we only had a single dollar between us. I told Jenny I'd be back in an hour. She said something to me in Chinese. I guessed it was, "Don't worry."

The previous afternoon, walking east we passed buildings under construction. I headed back toward Federal Highway for maybe a quarter mile until I came to a crew of construction guys working in the front of a building. I turned down an alley to the back of the place and sure enough there was a large garbage bin filled with refuse. Lucky for me the bin wasn't very high and standing on a cinder block I was able to climb inside. I began look-ing through a mixed-up tangle of old, crushed sheet rock, broken boards, discarded lighting fixtures, empty paint cans. Stuck under the mess were sheets of plastic that workers used when they were painting. I tugged fifteen or twenty feet of the plastic material free from underneath and gathered it in a messy roll and tossed it out of the bin. When I carried it back past the front of the building, one of the workers noticed me carrying paint-smeared plastic sheeting, shook his head at the kinds of junk bums carry off.

When I got back to the pier, Jenny seemed to be dozing with her hands fallen onto her lap. She looked okay so I didn't wake her. I stepped down onto the beach and noticed that the first thirty or forty feet under the pier was obscured by tall beach grass. I walked through the stuff and quickly shoved the plastic sheeting beneath the pier where it wouldn't be noticed and hustled back down Atlantic to the supermarket. The shipping cartons were still there leaning against the garbage bin. I took three of them and when I got back to the pier with the cartons, Jenny was still in the same position.

That's when I went back through the grass on the beach and took a good look beneath the pier. It was a place where a bum might crawl in to die. It was sickening with the stench of fetid mud, rotting horseshoe crabs, fish carcasses tossed from the pier, rotting seaweed along with beer bottles, and used condoms. Probably hiding in the mess were brown spiders. They are the scourge of homeless in Florida. I'd once been bitten by one. The bite doesn't hurt so much but the pain builds by the hour and soon you get a sack underneath the bite. It must be lanced before you get a bad infection. If a homeless guy goes to a corner medical clinic, they just cover it up with a bandage and send you away. You must go to the emergency room and start ranting you were bit by a recluse spider.

I got on my hands and knees, started gathering crap and tossing it closer to the water's edge. Then I tore one of the cartons making a scraper, and I started clearing away the muck and weed, trying to get down to fairly clean damp sand. After I had an eight- or ten-foot square half decent, I retrieved the remaining cardboard and spread it out to make a false floor, and once that was in place I unrolled the plastic sheeting and covered the cardboard with a blanket, tucking in the edges like a fitted sheet to keep our bed clear of moisture and hopefully to keep the spiders off us. This must have taken me an hour or more. Still our place wasn't the Marriott and I hoped she wouldn't be appalled and run off.

I was an unspeakable sight when I crawled out onto the beach. I'd worn the safari jacket for years on the street—the thing had kept me alive or so I'd imagined—but the jacket was finished and I tossed it into the garbage. I looked and smelled like a dark creature just arrived from Hades.

Jenny made a terrible face when she saw me, and then she laughed and pointed at the nearby men's bathroom where there were showers. There was even soap there. I scrubbed myself and put on an undershirt and shorts from my stash. I couldn't recall the last time I'd had on a pair of shorts.

Jenny was still sitting on the bench, arms in her lap. She smiled so beautifully and then showed me that tucked within the folds of her skirt she'd collected seven or eight dollars from sitting mournfully holding her little girl. Wow. What an unexpected score. Jenny didn't like to beg using her little girl. It was the only time that I ever saw her do it. She had been able to survive on the street as a dancer, but we were in trouble and she came through for us. I bought us cheeseburgers, fries, and shakes, and we ate our feast watching the last daylight from the pier, a special time.

When we finally made our way through the beach grass and ducked beneath the pier, it was too dark to see much, and anyhow we were both exhausted and fell asleep to the sound of a calm ocean lapping against the shore.

~

I woke a little before dawn and walked out onto the beach. There were pelicans mixed in with hundreds of pigeons wheeling above the surf in a kind of celebration of dawn. If you live on a beach, you get to witness this most mornings. I walked up on the boardwalk to a little stand selling coffee and had enough change to buy us two with a lot of milk.

She was awake when I got back, and after we had a few sips of coffee I pulled a pencil and the yellow pad out of one of the duffels. I wanted to start our work before the wharf grew noisy with tourists.

"I want to teach you some words," I said writing some words on a page. "Soon you'll be able to read." But Jenny looked distracted. How could she not be? We were lying beneath a gigantic pier, not unlike reclining underneath a bridge but without the traffic noise and fumes.

"Thanks so much," I said a couple of times, trying to catch her attention, and then I wrote it on the pad.

"I really appreciate your help. You can say this after someone helps you. I appreciate that you came with me on this trip to the ocean."

"Excuse me." "I'm sorry." "What do you think?" I wrote a few more phrases and coaxed her to repeat them, but she couldn't focus. Then I remembered how we'd started to understand each other the first day in the park. I moved a little closer to her, my hand barely touching hers. She smiled at me. I couldn't believe we were here alone under the pier. I was more than twice her age. My body was withered, and with my tangled white beard I could have passed for eighty. But I nervously took her little hand in mine, and after about a half minute I could feel her become more soft and yielding. She leaned over and kissed my cheek. I cannot describe how enthralled I felt.

"Excuse me." "I'm sorry." "What do you think?" I repeated these phrases and carefully explained what they each meant. Then she repeated them after me. They were only barely recognizable in her heavy accent that somehow made them more exciting. In a little while she took the pencil away from me. She wanted to write the words herself, and I soon saw why. She wrote the letters beautifully, like calligraphy. She loved the way the words looked and perhaps cared more about that than what they meant.

After a couple of hours of this, we ducked out from under the pier and headed toward McNab Park. I was curious to see what was going on there and if it was a place we might enjoy passing some time.

~

Coming from the ocean, McNab Park, bordered by warehouses and sundry buildings, feels claustrophobic and the air has a slightly rank smell. In the afternoon the windless landlocked park is miserably hot. Many of Pompano's homeless congregate here by day, and at dusk they move off for the night to vacant lots and alleys around Pompano. If you try to sleep in the park, you'll be locked up for vagrancy. You might wonder why homeless are drawn to this far less than wonderful park. There is no easy answer. I guess it is just one of the places that over time has accrued a vague feeling of home when you no longer have a home.

Soon after Jenny and I carried our duffels into McNab, we were greeted by Wayne, a tall, muscular guy with blue eyes and long blond hair. I had met him a few times in the park in Miami Beach where he sometimes came to visit friends. Wayne had a reputation as a fierce brawler. His mere presence evoked respect, and I never once saw Wayne challenged. "I used to watch Ralph talk to a lot of people," Wayne said to Melony, whom I soon learned was his girlfriend. "Bums really like to talk to Ralph. He knows a lot."

Melony, about thirty and nice-looking, was listening closely. "He's okay," Wayne continued. "He just talks to people. And his girlfriend isn't attached to reality, but she's not going to hurt anyone."

I was surprised Wayne knew anything at all about Jenny. I couldn't recall him being around during the days Jenny had moved into the Miami Beach Park. But there are networks among the homeless all up and down the state, and news travels. Wayne then moved off and began to chat with someone else. It was clear he wanted me to speak to his girlfriend, whom I soon discovered was the decision maker here. I wanted Jenny to be comfortable spending afternoons in this park and perhaps to have a friend, maybe to befriend Melony. But this was difficult because no one could understand a word Jenny said and she appeared to be living in a world of her own. I did my best to ease the way for her.

"This is my friend Jenny," I said to Melony. "We hang out together under the pier. She is very gentle and quite smart. But I should tell you she has an imaginary child. This is something you can go along with if you don't mind." I was a little nervous saying this around Jenny because she senses deeply, and I didn't want her to think that I didn't believe in the reality of her little girl. The truth was after a couple of weeks living with Jenny, I half-believed in her daughter myself, but Jenny didn't seem to notice what I was saying. Her eyes were running all around. I often wondered where her mind traveled when she was distracted like this. I worried she would wander off and that would be the end of it. "We're good people," I said, searching for the ticket into this place. By the seriousness of Melony's expression, you might have thought we were interviewing to get into Harvard. "You won't have a problem with us." I promised. Then Wayne looked at me and smiled. And I smiled back. "And Ralph won't talk behind your back." Wayne said to Melony. He's good people. Let's give him and the Chinese girl a chance."

Phew.

Wayne and Melony were the power couple here, but Melony called the shots. I would soon learn that she was stunningly intelligent. Melony was the arbiter of which homeless would be allowed to spend days in the park and who would be turned away. The setup reminded me of the wives of department heads in small colleges weighing in on new instructors just joining the faculty. Melony was looking for people to meet certain social standards. For example, you must not commit crimes when you are in this park. Do it somewhere else. You don't snitch people out or brown-nose the police. Not here. She didn't seem to care if you did strong-armed robberies in Broward County but not in McNab Park or with people with whom she and Wayne associate. One guy who spent many afternoons here robbed the weak and helpless all over Pompano, but in McNab he was always a gentleman. He was affable around all of us and was especially polite to the women. This was not a one-and-done admission process. Melony was aware of how you spent afternoons in McNab Park. If she turned against you, Wayne would make sure you never came back here again.

~

Many evenings Jenny and I enjoyed watching people fish on the pier. Some dropped simple handlines or cast out their baits with spinning rods. Others were deadly serious about their pier fishing and brought along custom-built carts with headlights for night fishing, rod holders with eight or ten rods in place, a large cooler for fish, a cleaning station, and many other gadgets. After sunset was usually the best time for fishing, and everyone was looking around to see what fish were being pulled onto the pier. It was a pleasure sitting there at day's end watching while a breeze off the ocean pushed aside the heat of the afternoon. When we were feeling hungry, I began looking into trash containers for discarded food for our dinner. There were so many people eating on the pier that glancing into the tops of large trash baskets it was easy to find mostly untouched sandwiches or fried seafood plates. Before bringing the food back to Jenny, I watched her sitting alone on the bench and tried to imagine what she was thinking about. Sometimes she snuggled with her little daughter or played games with her. Other times while I scavenged for food, Jenny sat there by herself as if there had never been any child. At these moments she seemed without purpose and almost without essence, as if a sudden brisk wind could blow her off the fishing pier into another man's dreams. Then what would become of me living under this pier?

But for the most part, the months by the sea were the happiest of my life, beyond happy, wherever that is. I thought we could make a beautiful life living here together. Okay, sleeping beneath a pier with crabs and spiders might sound like something Kafka would imagine, but with Jenny it was heaven. The night air sweeping in off the Atlantic was fragrant with dreams of our future together. The touch of her hand made me forget my age and lost life. We fell asleep to the sound of surf falling against the shore. Sometimes I would wake in the dead of night, and she was curled beside me holding her little one, and the lapping of the water rocked me back to sleep. In the darkness I felt as if we were sleeping on top of the ocean, slowly drifting east toward the Bahamas. We were so close to the islands I could practically see them from the end of the pier. I told Jenny that we would travel there someday, and she smiled at possibilities she could not imagine.

Each morning we sipped coffee while I taught Jenny simple English, and this teaching felt as important to me as working through dense philosophical jungles with Saul Kripke many years earlier.

"Great." "Fantastic." "Awesome."

"You can use any of these words to mean you like something. For example, Can I take you to dinner tonight? You can answer great, awesome, or perfect. It is like saying yes but more beautifully."

"When you meet someone and want to say you can't speak English very well, you can say I'm learning English or I'm just learning English."

I never knew exactly what Jenny was learning because in her voice, the words I taught her sounded like an altogether different language. We practiced saying the words over and over, but she continued to pronounce them in her own way. Sometimes she got annoyed with my corrections and wrinkled her nose. I gently pushed ahead with our lessons. Teaching her English was something I could give to her, but I worried if this work would bring us closer together or slowly push us apart.

~

One stormy night as waves pounded the shore, we felt salt spray on our faces and the lightning was blinding. The howling wind filled our darkness, and the rotting timbers of the pier creaked like an old sailing vessel in a storm. We were at sea in a gale and yet we were safe. I couldn't believe that before now I had spent countless lonesome nights beneath trees in parks or sleeping in alleys.

I turned to look at her in the lightning, and Jenny had taken off her long dress and folded it neatly on the edge of our cardboard and visqueen plastic sheeting bed. I could not believe she was doing this. How beautifully young she looked, so perfectly made. I couldn't take my eyes off her. "Very little," she said, fully holding her breasts in her little hands. I could barely breathe. I was so preposterously old and way past doing this. A lifetime past. I had no idea what I should do or if I should do nothing at all. Anything would surely be a blunder. Finally I managed, "I've forgotten how, Jenny." She smiled at me and took my hand.

~

Living in Pompano Beach began to feel like a normal life. Days in the park, I talked to homeless men, did my best to help. Then before sunset, I returned to Jenny and the pier, like a lawyer or an accountant, returning in the evening to the suburbs.

Few of my clients were practiced at talking about themselves. They didn't know how to do it and many were ex-cons and feared if they revealed information, it could be used against them. They often made declarations, such as, "He was wrong" or "He shouldn't have thrown my things into the street." Delving more deeply for these men loomed like a killing field. So a man would insist, "I was right. He will pay for this," or "I'll get even."

"Yes, I know what you mean," I might respond wondering what his life had been like growing up, what sorrowful path he had traveled to land in this stifling park. Then after some silence, or the next time we met, I might nudge him a little to consider what was behind all these declarations of right or wrong or of threatened retribution. More than once my client became enraged and raised his fist in my face.

"Look, we don't have to talk about this anymore if you don't like." Often he would walk off muttering to himself.

But more often than not, after a day or two, my client was back for another session, perhaps telling me that his mother was a whore or his father had no self-control and often beat him for no reason.

Then he might say, "I want to do more of this." He had begun to find our talks liberating as if some burden had partially lifted. Then we continued talking, uncovering pain and regret. Some men had been closed down for years and found the work exhilarating. Remember, talking is one thing you can do when you are homeless. You have all of this time to kill.

While I spoke with park regulars, Jenny sat on a nearby bench practicing her English words. Occasionally, when someone came by and spoke to her, Jenny answered hopefully with one of her new phrases we had practiced, but her accent was so heavy that people thought she was speaking Chinese and walked away looking perplexed. This always brought a smile to my face, and Jenny seemed happy enough studying her words.

One afternoon when there were no clients, I joined Jenny on her bench while she was snuggling with her little girl. They looked so precious together that I couldn't resist and bent over Jenny's arms as if I would kiss the little one, but Jenny stopped me with her hand and her expression turned icy. I had crossed a line I hadn't known was there.

As was the case in Miami, over time my park clients tired of our dialogue and some grew annoyed with me, having decided finally I was no sage with important advice to pass on, just another bum who had lost his home and was sleeping in back alleys.

But fuck it. I now had a girlfriend. And I was becoming skilled at something that I had known little about. I had come to realize that some who live for years on the streets had arrived at sincerity that is hard to find in normal life perhaps because so much on the surface has been torn away. Over the years, I had watched outsiders habitually stop by parks like this one and seem humbled by their talks with homeless men and women. These outsiders seem to think people here are privy to something they are not. Perhaps they are right.

I wanted to believe I was keeping Jenny alive, that I protected her and nudged her a few degrees toward a more practical reality, but at the same time, it was her untouchable essence that stirred me. I gave her what I had. I was so afraid of losing her. I dreamed of having money—I'd never cared about money, not really, but now I wished I had money, lots of it, so I could give it to her. I had nothing. Almost nothing. I tried to give her English.

"Jenny, if you don't understand what someone says, you can ask, 'Could you repeat that please?'"

"Repeating means to say the words again. Do you understand?"

"Anything is good," she answered with a big grin.

"Well, almost," I answered. "But better would be, 'Everything is good.' Okay?"

She answered with a wondering expression that left me puzzled.

Anything is good. Everything is good. Mine was surely more normal or I suppose, correct. But was it better?

I plowed ahead, writing phrases for her and saying what they meant. I couldn't tell how much of it stuck. She needed English to make it in the real world, to get off the street. That seemed to be the pot of gold for nearly everyone I talked with who lived on the street. But anything is good kept nagging at me. Jenny was getting at something else, something I hadn't considered.

I couldn't blame her for being distracted. Our underworld home had wild energy and many surprises. Under the pier we encountered feral cats, a whole colony, fourteen or even twenty of them. They must have been living here for years like the possums in the bushes near my clearing in Miami Beach. When we were sipping our coffee or studying English, they raced around distant pilings pausing to sniff the corpses of dead horseshoe crabs and snack on fish guts thrown from the pier. If we were still they came closer to take a look, trying to decide what we were doing in their damp underworld. We could see eyes flashing in the dark or shapes or shadows rushing past. Eventually one of the cats was brave and ventured over to our bed. It was a runty cat with no tail and a wounded body. She pulled along her frail back end. When I picked her up, she had no muscle or tendon I could feel. She felt like holding a damp rag. One day she came by when we were eating bananas and immediately started mewing for a bite. After this whenever we had a little money, we always brought her a banana on the way back from McNab Park. None of the other cats would touch bananas, but she loved them.

Jenny wrote to me on her yellow pad. "Dear friend, I want you to tell, I single mom. I am sorry before I am not talking you." I corrected her sentence and told her that she was doing great and soon everyone would understand her English. And this would change her life. She looked at me as if I didn't understand.

~

Usually in stormy weather, we were well protected under the pier, but if the wind was blowing hard from the north, the rain swept beneath the boardwalk and we shoved our bed to the south side of the pier to try to stay dry. In such storms, we got wet, but a few times I had some extra plastic sheeting, and we rolled up in it. Even in a full gale we were a lot better off here than huddled in an alley or a vacant lot.

Jenny loved ocean storms but really big ones now unnerved me because I feared losing a life I had just discovered. The waterlogged timbers made screaming sounds. What if the old pier crashed on top of us? Or what if a huge rogue wave rolled over us in bed and smashed us into the timbers or the concrete sea wall behind us? We'd be gone without a trace. But Jenny came alive in this weather. When the lighting flashed, her face was glowing. Big storms made her lusty, and while I pretended to be calm, she saw right through me, slowly pulled up her skirt, and tussled my hair. She knew I couldn't resist kissing her round belly until she grew impatient with me and pushed my head down between her legs. Storm be damned. Whenever there was a flash of light, I leaned up on my elbows so I could see her ecstatic face, and she would say strange endearing words that I could never understand or remember. I've tried so hard to remember those words.

In the morning I dragged our waterlogged cardboard and plastic sheeting bed out from under the pier, tore it apart, and put it in trash cans. Then I hunted around Pompano for cardboard boxes and visqueen plastic to build a new bed.

~

After a while, I grew tired of speaking to Jenny in gestures and simple phrases. I decided she understood me or I wanted to believe it. I would tell her all kinds of things.

"I'm interested in learning about you. As your English gets better, you'll be able to tell me more intimate things: what pleases you, what excites you, what saddens you, what big dreams you have. The small pleasures that make you happy.

"Learning about you will be a present for me. It's such a pleasure to know you, Jenny, to teach you, to talk to you, to make love to you . . . It's very hard to find someone you really, I guess, love . . . finding you was great luck for both of us . . . Don't you think?"

She smiles. I'm sure she understands. But if not, it doesn't matter so much.

One evening after returning from McNab Park, Jenny said to me, "I'm today, I worked so busy."

Without thinking I responded, "I think you wanted to say, I was so busy today that I am tired."

She nods and smiles while looking at a few small birds flying between the pilings just out of range of the cats. Jenny knew many words now but getting them into the right order seemed impossible for her. It occurred to me that perhaps her way, "I'm today I worked so busy," was more beautiful. Maybe I had it backward. I should be learning to speak in Chinese English instead of torturing her with proper English.

~

One evening, we were lying in our bed, watching the cats settling in for the night, when the pier above us began vibrating with rock 'n' roll. It was a hurricane of music, so we crawled out through the tall grass and walked up onto the pier. A rock 'n' roll band was playing on a shallow stage surrounded by a crowd. The band was a knock off of the Grateful Dead, though I did not know this at the time. But they were good, really good, and about a hundred people, many of them youthful drop out types, were smoking weed, singing along, driving the music.

Soon the band began playing "Scarlett Begonias." It's a song that drags you right into its simple beat and deep longing. I heard it the first time that night standing beside Jenny on this giant fishing pier where many thousands have come like pilgrims with rods and handlines hoping to pull a dream fish up onto the dock where we were standing in this gale of music. "Well, there ain't nothing wrong with the way she moves." The whole mass of people was swaying and singing, and Jenny began dancing in her bare feet, her Chinese rhythms stirred by rock 'n' roll and this song about a lady who could never be possessed. I tried to catch her eye to say, "Isn't this great?" but then I felt an idiot. I couldn't reach her and shouldn't have tried. "I had to learn the hard way to let her pass by. Let her pass by." She was dancing without shoes, and her movements were jerky and unkept as if defining beauty and rhythm from a different planet. The splintered old dock pasted with ancient fish blood was tearing her feet apart, but she was way past the pain or pain was part of what she was saying. Soon everyone on the pier was watching her. A teenage girl put a couple of small yellow flowers in Jenny's hair and she didn't notice, whirling on the old wooden planks, her face obscured by long, lustrous black hair. Her feet were filthy and bleeding, her forlorn dance paced with a touch of the blues. Do Chinese know about the blues? The crowd cheered and cheered and circled her and kept clapping as she danced in small circles. Stoners on the fishing pier fell in love with Jenny while she danced, and the guitar called to her in chilling eerie riffs. "Nothing wrong with the way she moved." It went on and on, twenty minutes, thirty minutes. It was an agony.

Stop, Jenny. Your feet are bloody. But no one wanted her to stop but me. Mostly with eyes closed, she danced her crazy Chinese rock 'n' roll. No one here had ever seen such a dance. When "Scarlett Begonias" ended, this strange lady would walk off and disappear and they would never see her again. None of them knew she was living with me right beneath the ancient fishing pier where they danced until midnight. I never felt closer to Jenny or further away.

~

One evening lying in our bed after sunset, I quoted lines to her from Dylan Thomas's "The Boys of Summer."

"I no understand," she said looking distressed.

"Listen when I say it again but don't try so hard."

I see the boys of summer in their ruin.

Man in his maggot's barren.

And boys are full and foreign in the pouch.

I am the man your father was.

She seemed to glimpse some of it, maybe the rhythm, but I don't know.

"It's not for you to understand. Try to feel the words like walking onto the pier in a storm, the wind and rain in your face."

Jenny smiled.

"Great writing means more than the meaning of words. Your dancing Jenny is like this poem by Dylan Thomas."

She shakes her head trying to reel in what I say but can't quite reach it. Then Jenny shivers and gives me a hug.

"It makes me happy to teach you. Why do you think it makes me happy to teach you?"

She hugs me again.

"I love it when we lie on our bed together studying English. After a while you put your beautiful naked leg over mine while you study the words, making a face to understand the present tense from the past. The present from the past are very hard things to understand."

She seems to notice that I shiver a little thinking about the present and past.

"You are so lovely trying to decide about time. Time is such a difficult question. I have wondered about this my whole life. Sometimes the present feels just like the past. I have discussed the present and the past for many hours with Bob Weingard."

She looks a little confused. Then she smiles. Then Jenny says to me, "Why I speak English so well to you? No one understands me but you?"

I can't think of the answer.

"Why you think?" she asks again.

"I don't know why."

"Maybe because hearts so close."

After a bit, I managed, "That's beautiful, Jenny. You see. The words can be more than words."

Long after I thought Jenny had fallen asleep, she turned to me and said, "I will miss you good teacher."

"I will miss you good teacher." She said these words in perfect English.

"Why, because you will leave me?"

"Yes, I will leave. Find millionaire for baby and I."

"Have you already met him?"

"Will tell you when."

I couldn't sleep at all that night fearing I had already traveled into the past.

~

Some mornings in McNab Park, Jenny sat on park bench by herself studying her English words. Most of the other park ladies had by now given up on her. I think Melony decided Jenny was crazy, mothering her imaginary baby and such, but Melony was always polite when she passed Jenny's bench, wished her a good day, and moved on. However, there was one lady, Martha, who was drawn to Jenny and seemed to be looking for her on the days she didn't come to the park. Both were outsiders and they didn't seem to need words.

Martha's boyfriend had been in prison for the past year for grand larceny, and she was lost without him. Before he was sent away, they spent months in the park together with Martha following five feet behind like a puppy. Her life now had become waiting for the day he would get out and come back to her. If he came back. Martha had been a beautiful woman but was forty now and living on the street had taken a toll. She walked miles trying to keep her figure for him. Each morning she visited the women's bathroom, examined her face in the mirror, grimacing at wrinkles and sunspots on her face before putting on her makeup. Sometimes I'd watch her speaking to Jenny but couldn't imagine what she said and how much of Jenny Martha could understand. Both were trying to fill a void. Once I watched Martha show Jenny a little makeup case, and she seemed to be explaining to her how to use it. Whatever they were saying I felt it was a great gift for Jenny to have a friend.

After we'd been living beneath the pier for half a year, Jenny only rarely came with me to the park. She needed time alone and I trained myself not to worry about her. We were happy living together and spending working days apart like many normal couples. Well, almost normal.

In the middle of summer after lunch, it was often too hot for heartfelt talks in the park. The homeless sat beneath trees positioning themselves best for a few inches of shade. Some afternoons, I passed time chatting with Melony who ran the show here as Wayne was often away drinking beer or smoking weed with buddies in Lauderdale or in some other park in Palm Beach.

Melony came from a working-class family in central Massachusetts. After high school she attended a technical school where she learned computer programming. She surprised her teachers with unusual speed and accuracy at this work and was quickly identified as a special talent. After a short apprenticeship with Data General, Melony was offered a position by a large Wall Street firm that used computers to do transatlantic securities trading. The company used large state-of-the-art NonStop computers made by Tandem that were delicate to work on and not completely reliable. Melany's accuracy, speed of calculation, and understanding of the equipment made her invaluable because screwups could very quickly cost the company millions. Within a year she was earning a six-figure salary.

Before my street life I had a good working knowledge of smaller computers. I knew how to build them and program them to work faster. And I knew something about the big machines from reading about them in magazines. But Melony had much deeper knowledge than I did, and she had a super-fast mind. I thought of technicians like Melony as gunslinger savants. It blew my mind to find myself learning subtleties of a technical subject I was well versed in from a lady who had been living in the street for years.

In the recession of 1987, Melony was laid off by her company and her life took a sharp turn. For a while, she worked as a waitress at an IHOP in Pompano Beach, then she met Wayne and quit her waitress job to live with him in the park. Melony might have gone back to Wall Street and earned a big salary. I wondered about that a lot, how seemingly immutable passions can wither or change shape.

After I knew Melony for a while, I proposed that she and I open a computer-related business in Pompano Beach and make good money. I reasoned that our complementary backgrounds could make us powerhouse consultants to small businesses in the area. Melony smirked and shook her head, no way. She never explained why. My guess was that cleaning herself up to start a business with me would have tipped the balance in her relationship with Wayne who had spent much time in prison for violent crimes and since then had gained a reputation as an enforcer in McNab Park. Melony adored Wayne and they had made a life together ruling the park and sleeping in an abandoned lot. I'd been hearing similar variations of the same story for the past twenty years. The homeless life is usually a one-way ticket.

I spent my days talking with the homeless in McNab Park for more than a year. To the best of my knowledge, no one there knew about Melony's earlier life and genius with computers besides me, perhaps not even Wayne. I guess it wouldn't have mattered much to anyone else. Melony might have been Mozart before she hooked up with Wayne and no one here would have cared.

~

I didn't think Jenny would ever dance again on the fishing pier to the music of the Grateful Dead band, but I was wrong about this. Each Tuesday night the band played above our home, and Jenny would walk onto the pier wearing a long, flowing white dress she'd stuffed in the bottom of her duffel. When she appeared, there was a thrill that rippled through the crowd like when the champ walks through the ropes into the ring. I felt it myself. On the second night she made her appearance, and on every subsequent Tuesday night, before she began her dance, Jenny put down a white bedsheet on the dock, poured black finger paint onto the sheet, and did her dance to "Scarlet Begonias" with her feet blackening the sheet into a Jackson Pollack abstraction much darker than the blues. She danced against the beat of the music, her hands swinging wildly, rising and then falling like a duck shot out of the sky, rising and falling pitifully as long as the band played "Scarlet Begonias" and the audience cheered and danced around her dancing, trying to copy her otherworldly rock 'n' roll. I admired her spirit but her dancing frightened me. I don't know why. When the band was exhausted playing her song and Jenny was soaking wet through her long white dress blackened with finger paint, people put many dollar bills on the sheet, and we had enough money for the week, more than we ever dreamed of having. The money was nice I suppose, but each Tuesday I felt unsettled while she picked up the dollars at her feet.

Jenny traveled her own way, like in the song, but always sensed my unhappiness and held me close as we fell asleep in the blackest of black nights beneath the pier.

The next morning at dawn, before anyone was around, we skinny-dipped in the sea and washed out the sheet and the white dress so it would be ready for the following Tuesday evening, and any bad feelings that lingered were quickly washed away in the surf.

I've often wondered if anyone ever saw us crawling in or out of our home, but if anyone ever did, we never heard anything about it.

~

Beneath a fishing pier is not the cleanest place. People are always throwing things down from the pier—beer cans and half-eaten food, paper plates, rotting bait—and many carcasses of fish and also horseshoe crabs seem to come here to die. Once or twice a week I made it a point to get home early from the park, before Jenny arrived from her travels, to clean the place and take a fast swim. Jenny had started wearing new clothes, skirts and slacks, lovely blouses she must have bought in a department store in Fort Lauderdale. I wanted the place to be nice for her.

This was our home. We felt like we owned it, although I knew we were breaking a homeless rule. Street people always take their things when they leave a sleeping place in the morning lest another homeless person take over the space. But our home beneath the pier amid the cats and crabs seemed golden, and I just didn't believe this could happen to us.

Whenever she was late getting back to Pompano, I waited for Jenny on a bench at the far end of the pier. After sunset I liked to watch the seabirds plunging into the ocean above small tuna that surfaced to feed on schools of bait. It was beautiful to see the tuna splashing at dusk just beyond the reach of bait casters who would die to catch one.

But a bigger thrill for me was to watch Jenny emerge from the fishing crowd, walking toward me on the long pier as if in a dream, her mind off somewhere I would never know about.

"I'm today I worked so busy," I said to her when she arrived just before dark. She nodded but didn't take me to task for speaking Chinese English. She was thinking of other things. When she sat next to me, I tried to kiss her cheek, but she turned her face away. "Not now," she said sternly. Soon she reached into her new handbag and showed me a bottle of face cream she had bought with a French label. She held it like treasure. "Put on my face." After this, whenever she put on her face cream, she wouldn't let me kiss her face or even touch it as if a finger might damn the restorative work of the potion. I understood that my lady friend was wearing the cream to look her best when she was out searching for a millionaire husband. But this new quest soon folded into our lives together where other things remained the same or were even better.

Many evenings after dinner Jenny invited me to kiss her belly. After a minute or two, she would stop me to tune her new FM radio to a blues station she'd discovered; then she'd settle back for a while on her duffel, and while I kissed her thighs and vagina, she'd repeat in a barely audible whisper, "I love you, I love you good teacher, I love you good teacher." Finally she would grab my head to stop, greet me with an endearing smile and ask if I wanted her to make me happy. Are you kidding? She made me feel like a teenager.

I learned the new rules. I must not kiss the invisible child resting in her arms or speak to her in Chinese English, though I wanted to. I could not kiss her on the cheek but was welcome to kiss her belly and her pussy. Jenny had a big hunger to be touched and a fear about being touched too much, a tangle of preferences and fantasies that made me crazy with passion.

After I had caught my breath, Jenny said to me gravely, "When I a married lady, you can't make love to me anymore. Not fair to him." When I nodded sadly, she added, "But sometimes I visit you under pier and still can make you happy good teacher."

"Wow, really? Will you do this?"

She nodded yes.

I believed her but if it wasn't true it didn't matter, such a charming thing to say.

Though I was not allowed to speak like she did, Chinese English remained the background music of my life.

"No anything is wrong." "She's at here." "I am they are good." "I am today I worked so busy." "I eat a lot food very day." "I want everything about me tell you." "Cruzy." "Cruzy!" "No anything happened" "I am so so sad." "Probably I am not with you eat dinner tonight" "But you and me will still in heart." "Anything is good."

She kept buying more beauty products.

"But you would be beautiful, Jenny, if you never used these."

She smiles but won't let me kiss her face. I pull her pants down a little and kiss the top of her pubic hair. She allows this, but not the face.

"Jenny, I love the way you smell. It excites me."

"Cruzy," she says, and lifts her arm for me to take a whiff.

"I think we're both a little crazy."

"That's why we have such good time, laugh so much."

Nights and mornings beneath the pier filled my life with laughter and wealth my father could never have dreamed of. With Jenny, who could not speak a proper sentence, I felt for the first time that I was understood. More than with my superstitious mom, who felt things deeply but not me, not really, and my sister, whom I adored but who thought I was nuts. More even than with Jean, whom I loved but needed to pretend I was a panther for her to really care about me. Jenny surely understood me better than Saul Kripke, whom the *New York Times* called the most intelligent man alive, and I wondered if within the fathomless depth of his logic Kripke could fathom such a love. For moments in a difficult life, I wasn't straining to bridge the gap between me and someone, anyone else. This woman who did not speak English was able to feel Ralph, and I began to feel him myself. I felt like I was discovering Ralph. Was it true? How can one ever really know such things are true and lasting but that was how I felt.

~

Jenny had much more money than she earned dancing for a half hour once a week on the pier. I never asked her about the money, but probably she worked part-time in one of the Asian spas in Fort Lauderdale. She was young and gorgeous and any man would have wanted her. But this didn't bother me much. We had a rich life together.

Once every week or two, I took a bus from the park to meet Jenny for a date night in Miami Beach or Fort Lauderdale. The first time we did this, I decided to bring her to the Chinese restaurant on Collins Avenue that I used to visit regularly with Jim when we were working the Fort Lauderdale garbage dumpsters. It had been a couple of years since I had visited this massive dumpster, and I figured surveillance would have died down and it would be safe to go back in. This huge restaurant had a big turnover, and there was always great fresh food in that container. Jenny and I arrived after dark, and we walked down the alley with its intoxicating smell of pork dumplings, Peking duck, and spareribs. But I had forgotten the vast height of the dumpster, and when I came alongside it, the thing was towering. I realized I could never get in there, even with a cinder block and a boost from Jenny. Jenny barely hesitated. She walked right over to the kitchen door and began knocking, signaled for me to go around the corner and stay out of sight. Ten minutes later, she was back on Collins Avenue holding two large-sized white containers filled with dumplings, shrimp, and lobster sauce with fried rice. I asked how she got the stuff and she said that she knocked on the door, smiled at the man in the kitchen, and asked politely. Wow. But who would ever turn her down? Jenny was a knockout.

Once or twice, we went to Ruth's Chris Steak House on North Federal Highway, which had the best steak and roast beef in Lauderdale. I knew Jenny could have knocked on the door to the kitchen, but she could sense I wanted to provide for her and the dumpster here was a shorty, only four or five feet off the ground. I managed to tumble inside, but it was pitch-black in there, and I didn't have the finesse of the homeless guys that were great at picking out the best in the dark. Eventually, I was able to find us two mostly untouched pieces of rare roast beef and a couple of baked potatoes. We ate it on a bench waiting for the bus back to Pompano, but I was a horrible mess from crawling around in the grease and swamp of gravy. Before crawling back under the pier, Jenny made me strip and swim in the ocean to clean up.

Those date nights in Fort Lauderdale, we ate like celebrities. Most of our food was fresh and hardly touched. I suspected that Jenny had the money to pay for some of our meals, but I never asked her, and I think she knew that I wouldn't have felt good about it.

I eventually learned a little more about the requirements of the millionaire Jenny was looking to marry. Her husband would be considerably older than her because she felt more comfortable with fatherly men, but she did not need to love him. She was very pragmatic about the millionaire. He would give her an apartment high in one of the new condominiums that lined the beaches of Miami Beach and Fort Lauderdale, she told me. It would be a spacious place with an ocean view just for her and the little girl. She wouldn't want him to live with them, but she would invite him to visit.

After several days or a week, when I could no longer restrain myself, I'd ask her, "Have you met him yet?" and she always answered, "Will tell you when."

The thought of her search made me shiver with sorrow or maybe it was admiration. A lost Chinese lady who could hardly make herself understood. There was something mythic about her quest that made it impossible to trifle with.

~

In the early afternoon, people in the park stood up and started slowly moving. No one talked about where they were going but everyone knew. You just got up and started shuffling ahead. If Wayne was off with his buddies, I sometimes walked with Melony, but usually I went there by myself. Unless I was distracted by something, I went most days.

We walked to the northwest. Those of us from McNab Park merged along the way with other homeless from nearby areas. About a quarter of a mile ahead, I could see a line of people looking like survivors of a tragedy slowly climbing a hill. It was sweltering hot, and I'm thinking I'm walking up a long steep hill to get something to eat. The afternoon heat was astonishing. But this was my crowd. All of us walking with determination, to get some free food.

The homeless mission was old and horrible. It reminded me of an insane asylum in a horror movie I once saw that specialized in lobotomies. It was filthy and falling apart, the furniture fixed to the floor like in prison. There were bugs everywhere. But for a free meal, most days I tramped over there and back in the heat. It was part of the life here.

After the meal, most of us walked back to McNab Park and other homeless areas, but a few who were flush crossed nearby railroad tracks to stop by a beat-up shack where the proprietor sold crack and joints and small bags of weed to homeless customers.

When we were back in the park from lunch, men brought me their sorrow. I tried to give them a glimmer of hope. Jenny had given me a supply.

One afternoon I was sitting on my bench chatting with four

or five skateboard teenagers who often spent afternoons crashing around the benches and on the lip of a broken fountain. They were school dropouts, trying to figure out the meaning of their days. Occasionally they would stop by to chat, probably because they were bored and had seen others talking to me. I worried about these kids who didn't seem to have much of a future and figured they'd end up in parks like this one or worse. I was talking about computers as a way to make a good living. One of the boys asked how to get started in the business and I said, one way is you could enlist in the army, learn computers there and when you get out it should be easy to find a good job.

It was then I noticed Martino within earshot. I knew him a little. I knew he had had been in the army, so I called out to him. "Hey, Martino, I've been speaking with these boys. Why'd you join the army?"

"Well, because I wanted to kill people," Martino answered. "The army was my opportunity to do what I wanted."

That ended the conversation, the boys exchanged glances and took off on their boards.

I had casual knowledge of Martino and his friend Bianchi, who seemed to detest each other but like a dangerous habit they stuck together for years moving up and down the coast visiting different homeless parks. They were both heavy drinkers and their jousting had a rancorous edge. "Watch yourself, man, one night I'm gonna slit your throat." Or "I'm gonna cut your balls off." Okay, homeless palaver, but sometimes an idle threat becomes real in the terrible heat of an afternoon in a park of sullen men. I tried to steer clear of these guys, but one evening, I ran across Bianchi coming my way as I walked back to the pier. He said he wanted to ask me a question. I nodded okay and we both walked into an alley. He then shoved me against a wall, pushed his knee hard into my groin, and made it clear I was going to come up with something or else. I wasn't a fighter. And if I was badly hurt, what would become of Jenny? She'd be afraid sleeping alone beneath the pier. I gave Bianchi what few dollars I had. That was it. After this, whenever I ran across him in the park, he gave me a friendly nod. It really hadn't mattered so much. It was a small event that blended into the heat of that summer.

~

Time had a different quality for me when I was with Jenny. Although we did little, I felt like we did so much. I realized that part of my desperate love for her was my own mutability that I felt now more than ever before. I'd been homeless for twenty years and I figured to die on the street. But she made it worthwhile. No one could have it better than nights beside her feeling the sea breeze under the pier, watching her dance in her own world with yellow flowers in her hair, eating for free from the best restaurants, even watching her going off with her baby into the big world, filled me with pride—a least one of us was trying to climb into a better life.

One evening I asked Jenny about her days in Fort Lauderdale, and she told me that she was spending afternoons in a park with some other single mommies and their babies. It was so gracious of her to say this to me, and for a time I stopped thinking about the millionaire. I enjoyed daydreaming about Jenny sitting in another park to the south among babies and their mothers speaking of the hard life and joys of single moms and Jenny's happiness having such a connection.

Her baby had become our secret sharer. Though I wasn't allowed to speak to Jenny's little girl or kiss her or even to ask questions about her, she was always with us. The little girl was a part of Jenny and almost a part of me. There was a time when she was having fevers and Jenny was bereft and I couldn't calm her. I held her and promised the little girl would soon be better, and soon that passed and Jenny's relief calmed me down.

One night after we'd made love, Jenny said to me, I have the pussy of a little girl, which set me back, and when I asked her what she meant by this, she turned away from me and went to sleep with her face tucked into the face of her daughter.

~

One day after Jenny stopped coming with me to McNab Park, her friend Martha came by my bench to talk. Martha had been missing her boyfriend for more than a year and now felt trapped. Maybe she should start fresh, move away from McNab Park, but like the rest of us, she didn't know which way to go.

"He didn't answer any of my letters," Martha said to me. But she didn't seem in despair. Maybe bored and fed up and trying to figure out where to go next in life. I really liked her. She always told the truth.

"Life in prison is a different thing," I said to her. She nodded while I told her what I'd learned from brief stays in Miami-Dade County Jail, which was a small prison, but mainly from years of talks in the park with ex-cons.

"His life is fully inside those walls. His range of options are contained within a courtyard and sometimes in that yard he might be chained by the ankles to other prisoners. Here we could go anywhere. There can be so many choices that it is unnerving, and it feels like anywhere is nowhere. But you could walk away from this park, Martha. You really could. In prison, he can't do that."

"After you've been inside awhile, you can't connect with the other reality. It disappears. It is like you've been corresponding with him in a different language. That's why he isn't writing. . . . When my friend Louie came out of prison after three or four years, I met him his first day out. First thing I walked with him to a nearby McDonald's and I bought him a big Mac. The guy took a couple of bites and began crying, really, crying, with tears coming down his face. Finally, he said to me, "This is the first meal I've had in years that has flavor." So that's why you're not hearing from him . . . he can't relate to anything that was before right now.

"Where should I go?"

"It's a problem for us all, Martha. Where you live is wherever you are."

When she stood up from the bench, she asked, "Why isn't Jenny coming by anymore?"

"I never know what she is thinking."

Martha laughed a little.

~

A few days later, after we were all back from lunch, Martha came by my bench holding two jumbo cans of beer. We walked together a short distance to the drawbridge over the Intracoastal on Atlantic Boulevard, sat beneath the bridge on cobblestones that were filthy from cars and trucks passing overhead but who cared about that when you were smoking weed or drinking beer at dusk by the water. Homeless like to visit this place. The police didn't bother us when we spent time under the drawbridge. Martha and I talked a little and then fell into the trance of early evening by the water-way. Soon we heard music coming from a large sailboat that was standing by north of the bridge waiting for the bottom of the hour for an opening. Martha started dancing a little to the music. After a minute or two she pulled her shirt off, smiled at me, and danced slowly in the shadows of the bridge. Her breasts were youthful and lovely. She laughed a little and came closer, wanted me to look at her. I said to her, "Martha, you are so beautiful. Don't worry." She smiled and kissed my cheek and after finishing our beers, I walked back to the Pompano Beach fishing pier and Martha headed west to a vacant lot where she spent nights with several others from the park.

~

One evening after dinner, while we were seated on the pier watching fishermen cast out their lines, Jenny handed me a note to read. It was in her handwriting, but it wasn't written in Chinese English.

Dear friend,
I am very grateful for your presence in my life, helping me and teaching me English. I will never forget you for the rest of my life, and I will always miss you.

"Who wrote this for you, Jenny?"
She shook her head no.
"Why? Because you will leave me?"
"Yes I will leave."
"Have you met him?"
"Maybe. Will tell you when."

But as the summer passed, she stayed with me beneath the pier, and I assumed that whomever she met had disappointed her. I only occasionally corrected her English, only when Jenny reminded me that she must learn proper English. I never knew where she came from in the evening or where she went in the morning. I sensed that I must not ask or she would disappear like a bubble.

Jenny's little girl rarely spoke, and when she did, she whispered in her mommy's ear. I wondered what she was saying, but Jenny would never tell me as if they were the deepest truths of the world, deeper than the solution to the sorites paradox, and she was afraid I would take her little girl's secrets and share them with the world and that it would ruin her daughter's life. I tried to constrain myself, but once when my curiosity got the best of me and I asked Jenny a question about her child's education, she closed the door fiercely and I felt afraid she'd leave me in the night.

In the morning Jenny was still angry and while she dressed, she told me she was no longer my girlfriend anymore, just a friend. I felt obliterated by this marker. Our love making had been the sweetest thing I had known in twenty years.

I thought this was surely the end of it. She had been preparing to leave me for the millionaire from the day she traveled with me to Pompano Beach. How could she live a life with a little girl and a ruined old man beneath a pier with feral cats, recluse spiders, and rotting horseshoe crabs?

But that evening Jenny came back to the pier smiling with her little girl trailing behind.

"You were so angry with me," I said to her. "I thought I would never see you again."

She took my hand tenderly and then hugged me while I tried to catch my breath. She began to kiss me, but when I forgot and tried kiss her cheek, she gently averted her face and reminded me she was wearing her skin cream.

"Sometimes I must be angry," she said in proper English and laughed a little. "It is nothing. Just something that happens. Anything is good."

I nodded yes. Anything is good.

"You always forgive me," she said. "Always encourage me."

I nodded yes.

"You will miss me someday."

"Yes I will miss you."

I realized now that Jenny could now speak perfect English or mostly perfect English whenever she wanted, and that in our fishing pier life she sometimes spoke Chinese English because it was our language and because it made me happy.

One evening five or six weeks later, Jenny returned to the pier wearing a black silk dress and smelling like French perfume. Mostly she spoke sentences in perfect English and then seemed to remember and said a few words the old way to relieve tension between us and elicit a smile. She hadn't danced on the pier in months, and when I mentioned it, she shook her head no in a way to suggest those days were in the past when she was young. More frequently, Jenny had been staying away for the night. We rarely ate dinner together anymore. I knew not to ask where she'd been, although in my head I asked all the things I didn't really want to know and that was enough to make her cross.

Then Jenny said to me once again, "Maybe I not be your girl-friend anymore. I be your friend, okay?"

"What will that mean?" I asked with my heart racing, and Jenny shrugged.

"It means I will still visit you sometimes. You can give me the truth about life."

This time, I sensed she meant it. I tried to accept what she was offering. I was still her teacher. There was always a chance, if he disappointed her, she might come back. Older, rich men often become bored with younger women. A chance. I tried to summon my logical prowess, but I wasn't thinking very well. I still had so much more than I'd ever had before knowing her. I should settle for half or even twenty percent. It was the best deal an old man could ever hope to have.

Don't drive her away, Ralph.

Except the heartbreak showed at the edge of my smile. Jenny could smell my sadness and she looked disgusted.

"Maybe we should stop for a while. Live a different way. I have things I need to do. You know that. I need someone to help take care of my daughter. I need to move on. I can't be with you forever. I told you this many times. I told you this, Ralph. I can't be with you anymore."

All of this in the perfect English I had taught her.

I felt myself crawl into a small, dark place. I hadn't visited here for a long time. From inside, she was a blur even with my glasses on as if I'd forgotten how to see. I couldn't speak. I could barely hear. I was afraid to turn around. I was sure she had crawled off into the night with the child, went to the apartment above the ocean to be with the millionaire and I'd never see her again. I must have fallen asleep and dreamed that I was back in the park off Collins Avenue sleeping beneath a tree. My feet were cold. I was afraid the cats had become rats and would soon begin to eat my toes. Then I heard Jenny whispering to me in the dark. She drew close and pulled me against her little body. We both cried quietly for a while, and before I fell asleep, I knew she'd stay with me and we'd have our sweet life together beneath the fishing pier.

Then in the morning, she gave me hugs and kisses, like she

always did, and we left for our work like we always had, although walking back to the park I felt like I was a hundred years old.

That night, she didn't return to the fishing pier, which wasn't surprising because I had grown use to her staying away. The next night, she also didn't return. But Jenny had told me she would come back, and I believed her. On the third night when I returned from McNab Park and made my way through the tall grass and looked beneath the pier at our bed, there were two bums lying on our mattress, settling in for the night. I was stunned and kept staring at them in disbelief until one of them screamed, "Get the fuck out of here!" They would have beaten me to death, so I turned around, crawled out from under the pier without a word, and slept the night in an alley. I returned again to the pier the next evening and watched for her. I wanted to alert Jenny before she crawled through the tall grass with her little girl and crept under the pier. But again, Jenny didn't come.

The following morning, I returned to the park bench and started meeting again with the homeless. What other option did I have?

~

During my first week back, Martha stopped by my bench twice I think and asked about Jenny, but I didn't want to talk about her. I tried not to lose my composure and made up a feeble lie because I didn't know where Jenny was spending days and nights and I felt ashamed. Unworthy. Martha seemed to envy Jenny for her courage to move on in life, that's what I guessed. By now, people in the park knew that Martha's boyfriend was out of prison and had not returned to McNab Park. I should have told Martha the way I truly felt. It might have made her feel less alone. You know, I wasn't a real professional.

In the early afternoon, as if there had been a signal in the sky, we rose from benches or from lying on the dry grass. We slowly struggled up the hill for tasteless food and came back later exhausted. Each afternoon, again and again. I was sixty-five years old.

Two or three times after lunch, I spoke to Martino who came up with a plan for stealing old boat radios from a nearby boatyard where he worked part-time sweeping out leaves. Martino was certain that selling these old ship-to-shore radios would give him a new lease on life. Maybe he could go back to the Midwest and find his wife he said to me. He'd be able to do anything he wanted. He'd be free of this place. Martino asked me to be partners in this pathetic endeavor, to help him hide the radios once he had them, but I couldn't find the right way to persuade him not to do this. I'd given Jenny all the best words, and now I could no longer find them. I knew Martino would be arrested and thrown in jail, and that's what happened a week later. I guess I harbored hope she'd show up one day in the park, tell me about the millionaire, and we'd laugh about it and pick up from where we left off.

There was no more taking showers on the pier or cleaning myself in the ocean. I didn't want to see the Pompano Beach fishing pier ever again. I think I went six weeks without washing myself.

It seemed like nothing would ever happen again. Another day, another desperate climb to eat. Another tasteless lunch. This was my life. At least the summer heat had passed. I walked slowly back to McNab Park with Melony. She said a few things about computers. I said something. It was like vaguely recalling a past pleasure. Most of us walked back to the park, although Martha and a few others headed west across the railway tracks to the marijuana shack. I knew she was friendly with the man who ran the place, and she'd sometimes go there after lunch to smoke a joint.

When Martha was halfway to the shack, she changed her mind and came back across the tracks in the direction of the mission. Probably she'd decided to return to the park with the rest of us, her friends said. But then she changed her mind again, headed east across the tracks. She couldn't decide which way to go. When the train came around the bend blowing the whistle, Martha seemed paralyzed. Her back was to the train, and when the whistle blew a second time, Martha turned around and faced it.

~

People in the park were flabbergasted. Martha's death was all park residents were talking about until they fell into uneasy silence and wonder. She had been such a quiet soul. Back and forth across the tracks. It was a mystery. Whoever gets hit by a train? But suicide? Martha didn't seem marked by death like others in the park who sleepwalked through their days. I had believed hope was winning out for Martha. A lot of homeless get runover by cars crossing busy roads and highways, but no one gets hit by trains that come at you screaming down the tracks and blowing a whistle to wake the dead. It was so dramatic and strange. I wasn't crying though. I'd already been run over by Jenny.

A day or two later, people in the park were handing around a tiny article from in one of the local papers. It was just a few sentences about a homeless lady who died on the train tracks near the mission. Reading it gave me the shivers. Not a single word about Martha's sadness and courage. Likely the readers in affluent sections of Fort Lauderdale and Palm Beach didn't have much of a response because there was nothing here of concern, nothing that could touch them like a virus or murder or a recession. She was just a homeless lady who died on the tracks, but if you'd seen her under the drawbridge dancing in the evening shadows . . .

Then a week later, a man from our park who occasionally came to chat with me about all he'd lost went to lunch at the mission and after another terrible meal he threw himself on the tracks in front of a train. He was a quiet guy who kept to himself. This happened the same week summer heat had made an encore in our area just when we'd all been celebrating the cooler weather. Perhaps because of the oppressive heat not much was said about his suicide. It seemed even harder to stand up and walk up the hill to the mission than ever before. But we needed to eat.

The following month, a man who was living closer to Palm Beach ended his life sitting on the tracks. And several days later, another man from our park committed train suicide. The one to the north registered like a curiosity, he was a stranger, but the one from McNab Park was a body blow. He was a tough guy, always in trouble with the police. Though people here didn't like him much, his suicide was foreboding. Why had he done this? Train suicide had become part of our lives now like thirst and hunger. It was so odd that Martha, so understated and kind, would have triggered an event that seemed like the work of a poisonous cult leader.

I tried to talk against it with the men on my bench in the afternoon, but it was a hard tide to swim against and honestly I was not at my best. Men shrugged at my arguments and more than one said, but not a bad way to go.

Three weeks later, another man died on the tracks. It got me thinking about years earlier in Miami Beach in the park, just down the road from the Fontainebleau, this was years before Jenny, when I wasn't eating unless a bum passed me a half sandwich or an apple. Most afternoons in the summer, there were fierce lightning storms. From time to time, people on the beach were hit, but I looked forward to the lightning. Late in the afternoon, when it looked like storms were closing from the west, I would cross Collins Avenue to the beach hoping the storm would come my way. When the clouds darkened, the lifeguard on duty ordered everyone off the beach, but I stayed there by myself, right out in the open. I loved feeling the wild wind and the lightning flashing all around me. Sometimes I shouted into the storm, go ahead, kill me if you can. I did this a half dozen afternoons. It made me feel alive. I was like a kid accepting a dare. Kill me if you can. I didn't think of it as suicide so much as an act of defiance.

The articles in the local papers kept tracking the deaths,

although mostly they focused on the engineers of the trains, which made sense in a way because the homeless were anonymous, and I suppose to the general public, they were interchangeable. There were usually interviews with the latest engineer who had run over a guy sitting on the tracks. Some of these men felt remorse, and some were outraged that nothing was being done to stop it so they could do their work properly. It's just not fair, one man complained bitterly, I wasn't hired to kill homeless on the tracks.

While the suicides continued, Martha began to visit me in the night, only a voice speaking to me, more innocent and childlike than I remembered, but it was Martha. "There are certain things you do without understanding until afterward," she told me. "Like a bird building a nest without exactly understanding why."

Hearing her voice was reassuring to me as if we were still talking in the park, well, almost. Frankly, speaking to her helped me escape the pain of Jenny. Afternoons I waited for her on the bench to speak to me or to walk past with a wave as she had most afternoons before her suicide. She assured me, it was the right choice. "This is a better place for me, Ralph. You're the only one I speak to here." Each time I heard her voice, it was a relief from the tension of waiting for more awful news.

Then after about two weeks, Martha disappeared entirely, and I could no longer reach her. I tried to, but she was gone. The talks I had been having with homeless had given my life meaning for years, but now they had become useless. I was just hanging out in the park like other men waiting for the next one of us to jump in front of a train. Jenny was my girlfriend, but I yearned for Martha. I was in the grip of something I didn't understand. I tried to shake it off, but I couldn't.

THE END

Epilogue

As I wrote in the beginning of *Anything Is Good*, Ralph Silverman was, in fact, my best friend in high school. More than sixty years later, I asked Ralph how he felt about my writing a novel, a work of fiction, inspired by his astonishing life. He agreed, so this novel was seeded by Ralph's memories of remarkable events and people he had known. The characters I met through Ralph traveled their own way and introduced me to new characters. The stories Ralph told me led me to other stories that seemed to write themselves. I suppose this is the magic of a great muse, to lead a writer to the brink.

~

A reader might be interested to know what became of Ralph Silverman, the living, breathing antecedent of my character in the novel.

Nearly eighteen years ago, Ralph called me collect from a phone booth in Florida. I hadn't heard from him for two or three years. By then he had been sleeping in parks and back alleys for more than twenty years. Ralph had become an old friend from my distant past. I rarely thought of him anymore.

"Fred, I need to tell you something. I can't keep living on the street. I don't think I'll be alive much longer if I keep living like this."

That's the gist of what he said. I figured Ralph had become sick from years of bad food and living outdoors. I knew very little about his homeless life. I didn't know anything about Brandon and Bianchi or the Crips. This was many years before I imagined Jenny and Ralph loving each other beneath the Pompano Beach Fishing Pier. I had never heard of the song, "Scarlet Begonias." Probably if he had tried to tell me the plot of his life years earlier, I would have been too preoccupied with my own concerns and dreams to take it in.

The jolting prediction of his imminent death is the only thing I can recall about his phone call. I told him that I'd come down to Florida, and we'd figure out what to do.

I met him in Pompano Beach outside an old bank that had been closed for three or four years. Ralph was emaciated and black with filth, and he smelled horribly. For weeks, he had been sleeping open to the weather on a concrete sidewalk beneath a boarded-up teller's window. He picked up his duffel, and we drove a half mile to a Burger King for breakfast.

I made phone calls and found out we'd need to go to Broward County Human Services to find out what off-the-street options were available for an elderly homeless man. We drove to the welfare office and filled out many forms and were promised a phone call, but after several days, when there was no call, we went back to Human Services again, and then we went back there again and again. There were just too many homeless looking to get off the street and few places offering decent food and lodging. By sheer luck, on our fourth or fifth visit, Ralph was interviewed by a young social worker who had studied some philosophy in college and was simply astonished by this remarkably intelligent man who had been surviving storms, heat waves, and periods of starvation in parks and alleys for twenty years. Ralph eventually received a Section 8 voucher that would provide rental assistance from the state for safe housing in the private market.

~

For the last seventeen years, Ralph has lived in a tiny apartment on the second floor of a multi-dwelling unit in Fort Lauderdale, only a short walk from an excellent Taiwanese restaurant where he had once been lookout for the police while his friend David harvested from the restaurant's savory garbage container.

Using some of his social security money, Ralph built his own personal computer from scratch and began to research some of the newest writing on modal logic. He soon forged a relationship with a professor who taught epistemology at a local college, and they had long discussions about the early esoteric writing of Ludwig Wittgenstein and Bertrand Russell and their profound influence on the development of digital computers in the 1960s and ultimately artificial intelligence. This is a subject Ralph intended to write about, and still does.

~

But also, Ralph confided to me that living studiously and some-what conventionally felt deadening. "I began spending afternoons each week in nearby areas where the homeless congregated. I was immediately accepted in these places as a street guy. Homeless can tell. They can smell it. I soon met old friends from my past, Sandy, the rich girl who'd left Barnard for the park life in Miami Beach and who still claimed to have a boyfriend living in one of the opulent condos on the water, and Bianchi, who had beaten me up in an alley in Pompano Beach. Even as an old man, Bianchi made sullen threats, but I didn't mind. His crime stories made me feel edgy and woke me up.

"The homeless life is something I can't let go of, not entirely. During recent years, when my health hasn't allowed me to travel to homeless parks, my friends come to visit me. It's hard to explain this to normal folks. My whole life I've been a social amphibian, straddling between different worlds, never entirely comfortable in any of them. When I was a kid, I felt as if I were from a differ-ent planet and each day I needed to pretend to be normal to get by in school and to get along with my family. Living in an air-conditioned apartment today as an old man, I yearn for the violent summer storms, for the wild beating of my heart."

Acknowledgments

I wouldn't publish anything without first putting it past my wife, Bonnie, and my son, Josh. They are my most enthusiastic and toughest readers. I've worked with many magazine and book editors and often felt like I was in a losing tug-of-war, bartering over sentences and sometimes giving away good material that should have remained in the book. Bonnie is the only editor I fully trust. If a sentence of mine is awkward, she can fix it without compromising my sensibility or the rhythm of my prose. If I lose my way in the narrative, she bails me out with ideas that feel like my own. Really, she is a marvel. I could not write a decent book without her.

My son, Josh, is a powerful thinker, and his ideas have deeply stirred many people, including his dad. Usually, he only makes a few remarks about a manuscript but they leave a mark. Josh read an early draft of this book and recognized an unevenness in the first chapters. We argued as we often do, but his critique got under my skin and I went back and chiseled away until I fully understood what he was getting at and finally I think the opening pages became the gateway the novel needed.

As I've written in the epilogue of this book, *Anything Is Good* is a work of fiction inspired by a true story. Without the astonishing history of Ralph Silverman, there would be no story here to write.

Many authors have in mind a small group of readers they most want to hear from about a newly finished work. I sometimes feel as if I am writing the book for these few.

Besides Bonnie and Josh my earliest readers of this work were Chris Begg and Richard Friedman, both of whom inspired me with their encouragement. For years, I have shown early drafts of my books to thoughtful readers: Melinda Mathews, Hannah Beth King, Barbara Stapleton, Bruce Pandolfini, Aiden Slavin, Luis Palcio, Alex Twersky, and Emilio Nunez.

Jay Bergen, your counsel was hugely important and I cannot thank you enough.

Kanami Kusajima, your thrilling and utterly original dancing in Washington Square Park inspired the pier dancing of the character Jenny.

Mary McAveney, I cannot thank you enough for your sage advice about how to best bring this novel into the world.

Thank you, Mara Anastas, for believing in my novel and for your many suggestions along the way.

Lissa Warren, I greatly appreciate your thoughtful and enthusiastic work helping my novel gain a readership.

Emma Chapnick, you stayed on top of so many details with a steady hand and always with a relaxed encouraging manner.

Mauricio Díaz, you have designed three beautiful book jackets for me. When I first saw the cover for *Anything Is Good,* it took my breath away.

Open Road has produced the most beautiful-looking books for me and made the entire publishing process a delight.

Some sentences on pages 89–92 were paraphrased from a piece I wrote for the *New York Times Magazine* in 1989 called "When All the Stars Are Gone."

About the Author

Fred Waitzkin was born in Cambridge, Massachusetts. His father, Abe, was a salesman and his mother, Stella, an abstract expressionist painter and sculptor. To the best that Waitzkin can recall, his parents never shared a warm moment. Early on, the young Waitzkin considered careers in sales, big-game fishing, and Afro Cuban drumming, but by the age of thirteen he decided he would be a writer. Both of his parents were strong literary influences, along with Ernest Hemingway: "His little sentences thrilled me with descriptions of men pulling in huge sharks and marlin."

Waitzkin was an English major at Kenyon College in Gambier, Ohio. During the summer vacation following his junior year, he met Bonnie on a sword fishing trip, and a year later they were married. Waitzkin received a master's degree at New York University and, for a time, considered pursuing a career as a scholar of seventeenth-century poetry. He taught English at the University of the Virgin Islands; however, he admits that it wasn't his love of teaching poetry that intrigued him about St. Thomas, but rather the rumors of thousand-pound blue marlin that were said to graze twelve or fifteen miles north of the island in a patch of ocean called "the saddle."

Following their St. Thomas years, the Waitzkins settled in New York City. After collecting a great many magazine rejections for his short stories, Waitzkin began writing feature articles, personal essays, and reviews for numerous publications including *Esquire*, *Forbes*, the *New York Times Magazine*, the *New York Times Book Review*, *New York* magazine, *Outside*, and *Sports Illustrated*.

In 1984, Waitzkin published his memoir, *Searching for Bobby Fischer*, about himself and his son Josh, a chess prodigy. The book became an internationally acclaimed bestseller. In 1993, the film adaptation was released by Paramount Pictures and, that same year, was nominated for an Academy Award.

In 1993, Waitzkin published *Mortal Games*, a biography about world chess champion Garry Kasparov. It has been described as "a remarkable look inside the world of genius—a brilliant exploration of obsession, risk and triumph."

In 2000, he published *The Last Marlin*, a memoir that was selected by the *New York Times* as "a best book of the year."

In the spring of 2013, St. Martin's Press published *The Dream Merchant*, Waitzkin's first novel. *Kirkus Reviews* wrote, "Waitzkin offers a singular and haunting morality tale, sophisticated, literary, and intelligent. Thoroughly entertaining. Deeply imaginative. Highly recommended."

His second novel, *Deep Water Blues*, published in 2019 by Open Road Media, is set on a remote and sparsely populated Bahamian island, where a peaceful marina becomes a 133 battleground. "This is like sitting by a fire with a master storyteller whose true power is in the realm of imagination and magic," wrote Gabriel Byrne.

Waitzkin lives in Manhattan and Martha's Vineyard with his wife, Bonnie, and frequently visits Costa Rica. He has two children, Josh and Katya, and two cherished grandsons, Jack and Charlie.

FRED WAITZKIN

FROM OPEN ROAD MEDIA

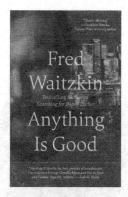

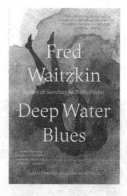

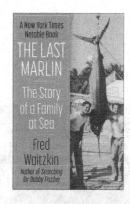

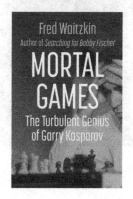

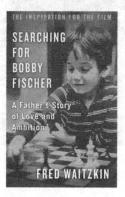

OPEN ROAD

INTEGRATED MEDIA

Find a full list of our authors and
titles at www.openroadmedia.com

FOLLOW US
@OpenRoadMedia